Richard F. Green was an actor in the late '50s and early '60s at Stratford and the Birmingham Rep. In the '60s, he graduated as a teacher in Hull. He formed his own theatre company and school in the mid-'70s and staged productions at the Royal National Theatre and the Edinburgh Festival. At the festival, he was responsible for mounting an original production on Myra Hindley and won 5-star reviews for his interpretation of Sondheim musicals.

Richard F. Green

BLOOD AND CONFUSION

AUSTIN MACAULEY PUBLISHERS™

LONDON • CAMBRIDGE • NEW YORK • SHARJAH

A CIP catalogue record for this title is available from the British Library.

ISBN 9781398417823 (Paperback)
ISBN 9781398417830 (ePub e-book)

www.austinmacauley.com

First Published (2021)
Austin Macauley Publishers Ltd
25 Canada Square
Canary Wharf
London
E14 5LQ

Daniel Sproates for his intelligent editorial advice.

Thanks to my cousin Jean for her hard and focused work, correcting the many spelling and punctuation errors in the original work.

Chapter 1

It's Raining Men

Tony's arm lay across Robert's chest. His brown and muscular arm, half Moroccan, half English, contrasted with Robert's white, almost delicate body. Both men were fit and manicured, their muscles well-toned and showed regular visits to the gym.

The two lads had been partners for five years and were thinking of making it legal. No marriage, that was out of the question, but a civil partnership seemed a possibility. It had been a good Saturday night in the club off Old Crompton Street. They'd drunk too many tequilas, had enjoyed being chatted up by good-looking young men, and had come home, as always, on their own. It was now Sunday morning, and they were sleeping off a hard night and what could turn out to be a big hangover, when the telephone rang.

'Who the hell is that?' moaned Robert.

'Maybe that lad you chatted up last night,' retorted Tony.

'I never gave him our address. Well, are you going to answer it?'

Tony stretched out his arm and lifted the receiver.

'Where the hell have you been? I've been calling since seven this morning,' cried a voice with a distinct Australian accent.

Tony put his hand over the phone to inform Robert that it was Dame Edna. Dame Edna was the nickname given to Mark Travis, the head of the North African desk of MI5. It was Mark's job to monitor any jihadist movement within the UK.

'Switch on your television,' he ordered.

'What? Has mother broadcast another cookery programme?' quipped Tony.

'No time to be flippant. Put on the news channel and then come to see me. I'll expect you at eleven.'

With that order, he slammed the phone down.

'Your word is my command,' retorted Tony sarcastically.

Nevertheless, Tony put on the news channel and waited for the headlines, which were not long in coming. Three men, it said, had fallen to their deaths in what was considered a terrorist-motivated crime. The television then showed a man dressed in black Islamic robes, face covered, and screaming something in Arabic.

'What's he saying,' asked Robert, and Tony quickly translated.

'Basically, he's saying that it's a sin to lie with another man; it's an affront to the Holy Quran and Muhammad himself. These men, he claims, should be cast off a high rock into the valley below. He then goes on to say how things will be different when all mankind is ruled by the word of Mohammedan and Sharia law. I'd better get down to the office; by now there will no doubt be a red alert.'

Tony went into the bathroom and Robert into the kitchen to fix a pot of coffee and some toast.

Fifteen minutes later Tony was dressed and drinking a couple of mouthfuls of coffee. He grabbed a slice of toast, kissed Robert on the cheek, told him he'd meet him at the little Greek coffee shop near the British Museum at about 1 pm, and left.

It was a nice bright morning for October, so Tony left his apartment near the embankment and decided not to take the car, but to follow the Thames to MI5 headquarters at Thames House. There were few people out: a man with a dog and a couple of joggers, so it was a pretty normal Sunday morning.

Arriving at Thames House, he signed in and went to the fourth floor and directly to the office of Mark Travis. Mark was a very well-dressed man in his fifties, who sported a rather dashing pair of red designer spectacles, which added even more to his nickname of Dame Edna.

'So you're here,' he said disparagingly.

'Sorry I'm late, had to clean my teeth,' retorted Tony.

'So what do you think?'

'Well, he's not from North Africa.'

'Because?'

'Because his Arabic is not good. No doubt learnt the language in an Arabic school in England. Maybe his family is English. Places his vowels incorrectly.'

'Well, that's something. Sharia law on the streets of London. Where the hell has our intelligence been?'

'Nothing has been picked up. At least nothing of that nature.'

Mark continued to moan that the Home Secretary had been on his back.

'He was on the phone for half an hour. God, what an old woman he is.'

Tony raised his eyebrows. Mark said, 'Wants me to set up a team to look into this outrage.'

Tony looked puzzled. 'Surely the Met will be dealing with it.'

'And us. And us,' interjected Mark. 'All reports to me will go directly to the Home Office.'

'To the old woman herself,' Tony said grimacing.

'Exactly,' said Mark, not picking up on Tony's sarcasm. 'A special team and I want you to head it.'

'Me!' said Tony, rather shocked.

'Well, don't look so surprised. Wondered if it had any tie-in with the priest that was burnt alive.'

'No,' interposed Tony, 'the cell which engineered that atrocity has been closed down and the perpetrators now face heavy prison sentences.'

Mark grunted. 'Nevertheless, it would do no harm to check it over.'

Tony, not wanting to sound too self-deprecating, asked whether Mark really thought he was the right man.

Mark was emphatic. 'Exactly, after all you've already told us that he's likely to be someone born in the UK, that in itself narrows the field. You're exactly the right man. You speak fluent Arabic, got a first in Islamic Studies from London University, and you're queer.'

Tony cringed. Mark's lack of PC always took him off guard. He should complain, but in a sense, Mark used it as a means to be friendly, and was he offended? No. Not in the least.

'Your lack of PC amazes me,' smiled Tony.

'Well, you are, aren't you?' commented Mark, not really seeing the humour.

'As well as being an Oxford scholar and speaking fluent Arabic. Yes, I suppose you're right.'

Mark moved on, disregarding Tony's comments. 'You'll have someone joining you from the Met.' He announced in a manner that was not to be questioned. Tony could not, however, resist the dig.

'Is he queer, too?'

'How the hell would I know,' complained Mark. 'He's married with a couple of kids.' Mark looked through his file. 'Not that marriage and children counts for anything these days.'

'That's true. What exactly did he do in the Met?'

'He does have a name,' grumbled Mark.

'Well, that's reassuring.'

Mark looked through the file on the desk. 'Simon Newlove. Worked for the Met for five years in their forensic department, has a chemistry degree from Nottingham. 2.1: not bad. You don't need me to read the rest of this stuff.'

He pushed the file over to Tony. Mark suddenly picked up his phone and instructed his secretary to send Simon Newlove into his office. He then turned back to Tony.

'I thought having a scientist on board would be helpful. Knowing your loathing for blood and guts.'

Tony ignored the comment. 'He does understand that working here is very different from…'

Tony was stopped in his tracks by a stunningly good-looking man. *He was well-groomed, wearing an expensive suit, and obviously had just had his hair styled. I'd better keep this quiet from Robert*, was the thought that ran through Tony's mind.

'Ah, Simon, come in,' ordered Mark with a welcoming smile on his face. 'This is Tony, the officer who will be heading up the anti-terrorist team dealing with the rooftop murders. Tony, this is Simon.'

The two men shook hands and made the usual noises of 'nice to have you in the team' etc.

Mark ignored the niceties and ploughed on. 'The post-mortem is at 2:30 pm today. You can take Simon with you.'

'No,' replied Tony, 'Simon can go on his own.'

'Read too many Colin Dexter novels. Like Dexter's hero, he's squeamish when it comes to post-mortems,' carped Mark.

'I'll admit I don't like them, but I thought it would be better if I visited Mr Saleem Khan and revived past memories. Then tomorrow a brief visit to Mother to pick her brains regarding this case and how it may impact on the priest-burning case.'

Simon was immediately alerted. 'Priest burning?' he enquired.

Tony smiled. 'I'll explain later.'

Mark then told them that the Met had been informed of their involvement. 'They may be a bit frosty,' stated Mark. 'But they have been told in no uncertain terms that they have to keep you abreast of any developments. This, however, is not a two-way street. If they stray into areas of national security, you have the powers to close down their investigation immediately. After contacting me, of course.'

Sometimes Mark was outrageously smug. 'On your way out, tell Sarah to bring me in a large black coffee.'

The two men left the office and Tony greeted Sarah and introduced her to Simon. She smouldered with positive warmth at meeting this new handsome recruit. Then, with a big smile on his face, Tony instructed her that Dame Edna wanted a black coffee.

Chapter 2

Old Acquaintances

Tony had left his car at home, so opted to be driven to the crime scene in Simon's rather smart and very clean BMW.

'This is a rather expensive car, come from money, do you?' remarked Tony.

'Aunt died, left me some cash, so I thought why not?'

It took a little over twenty minutes to drive to the crime scene, which was in Chiswick. A Sunday morning meant the roads were relatively clear.

On the drive over, Tony was able to clarify his earlier remarks about a burning priest. 'It was some radical movement in the North of England. They kidnapped a village priest who spoke out against Islam. Took him to a field and basically set fire to him. The same way as we did to renegade Catholics in the sixteenth century.'

Simon nodded. 'Yes, I remember reading about the case.'

'My mother lives in the north near Pickering,' explained Tony. 'She and my father were both agents for MI5, that's how they met. When he was killed, she retired to the country, developed her passion for cooking, and now runs a weekly TV programme called Country Cooking for Beginners.'

'Gosh, is that your mother?' exclaimed Simon.

'I'm afraid it is,' confessed Tony.

'And is that where we're going tomorrow?'

'No, you're far too good-looking. She'd think that I'd ditched Robert for a new model.'

Simon grinned. 'Besides, you have to stay in the office and write up the autopsy report, Mr Scientist, in simple words that I understand. You could also find out all you can about the victims. Who they are, what they did, any past crimes, etc.? Robert? Who's Robert? Your boyfriend?'

'My partner,' corrected Tony. 'How did you know that I was…?'

'That you were gay. I did some research on you and other members of the company.'

Tony looked startled.

'It appears you're not the only gay in the village,' continued Simon.

'I don't wish to know,' Tony was feeling a little discomfort at his new partner's appetite for scandal.

'My best friend was, is, gay,' persisted Simon. 'And during my late teens and early twenties, I spent most Friday and Saturday nights in gay clubs. I preferred them to straight clubs. Better music, and the people were there to really enjoy themselves and dance, not get drunk and get into stupid fights.'

Tony agreed.

They drove down Knightsbridge, through Earl's Court and Hammersmith, and ended up in Wellesley Road, Chiswick, outside what looked like a 1920s block of flats.

'Very nice,' muttered Tony, who appreciated the Art Deco look. They went to the door of the flats, only to be stopped by a policeman. They flashed their warrant cards and were admitted. The lobby was pretty bare, but to Tony's relief he noticed that the lifts were not out of order. The flats were obviously private and well-maintained. They went up to the sixth floor, and then there was an extra flight of stairs which led to the roof. Loungers, tables, and summer chairs were neatly placed for the use of the tenants on summer days. 'Very nice,' reiterated Tony.

'Not what you expected, eh?' persisted Simon, with his amiable banter, which was beginning to irritate Tony slightly. 'Expected a rough council flat in Neasden. This all looks very luxurious, a bit Hercule Poirot. It's 1920s. But it's hard to imagine how he got three men to stand on the perimeter wall and then fall to their deaths. Must have been drugged.'

'Yes, drugged,' agreed Tony. 'But not all together. When you go to the autopsy, make a detailed check on the time of each death. I suspect they were brought on to this roof one by one, over, say, a thirty-minute period, and I would also suspect that the film was recorded before the murders took place.'

'If he did that, he was taking one hell of a risk,' retorted Simon.

'We'll take the staircase down. I want to make a closer investigation of the interior,' commanded Tony.

As they got near the bottom of the stairs, they met a sprightly elderly man struggling with his shopping.

'Let me give you a hand,' said Simon in a cheerful manner.

Mr Peters, the elderly man, willingly handed the shopping over. 'Only live on the second floor, hardly seems worthwhile using the lift.'

'Are the flats always as quiet as this?' asked Simon as they mounted the stairs, leaving Tony in the stairwell looking at the tenants' notice board.

'It's Sunday,' maintained Mr Peters. 'Besides, we're a crime scene. Some fellows fell to their deaths from the roof.'

'That's terrible,' chatted Simon. He was admiring the interior of the flats and the carpeted passages. Definitely not Neasden. 'Are the flats always as quiet?'

'Not always. Foreign chap on the fifth floor, always playing loud music and having parties. Mrs Peters has complained more than once.'

Tony had now rejoined them, and Simon, having handed the shopping back to Mr Peters, told Tony where the flat was that he thought they needed to see. Using the lift, they ascended to a very smart and well-kept sixth floor. Like the rest of the block, the interior passage to the flat was well-carpeted. At the door of number six, they were greeted by Chief Inspector Bullock of the Met, round-faced and with the look of a man who had just eaten a sour apple. He knew Simon and looked at him with contempt. 'Ah, Newlove,' he griped. 'I'd heard you'd crossed to the other side.'

'Better prospects,' retorted Simon.

Bullock sneered. 'Easier life, more like it. Well, I've been told we have to be helpful so you'd better come in. Not that you'll find anything. The place has been swept clean, unless, of course you like couscous. There's bags of the filthy stuff.'

Tony slipped in silently, ignored by Bullock, who was keener to continue making cynical comments to Simon and carp about his life in the Met. While their conversation went on, Tony looked around the flat. Not so much as someone inspecting a crime scene, but more as a prospective tenant or estate agent. It was a two-bedroomed flat with a spacious lounge. Metal windows that suited the curvature of the room. Sadly, the interior decor did nothing for the room's style. The bedrooms were adequate, and Tony thought that if he lived here, he'd convert one of the bedrooms into a dining room. The worst feature was the galley kitchen. I hate galley kitchens, he thought, but I guess you can't have everything. I wonder how much the rent on such a property would run at. Won't be cheap. Not in London and not in Chiswick, an area which still has an upper-class residential quality about it.

Bullock was still whining at Newlove when Tony joined them, dropping in an obviously relevant question. 'So this is where the three unfortunate men were before they met their deaths?'

'Seems like it,' said Bullock grudgingly. 'I bet when we get to the autopsy, we'll find they were full of drugs. A party that went wrong.'

'Oh,' remarked Tony with a look of irritation on his face. 'So they were full of LSD and they went onto the roof to see if they could fly.'

'Something like that,' sneered Bullock.

'And what about the man in Islamic dress? A fancy-dress party was it?'

'I haven't as yet received the correct translation.'

'No, but I have, and I can tell you now that this was no party.' Tony's irritation was at breaking point when he turned to Simon and told him that it was time to go.

'See you at the autopsy,' smiled Bullock.

'Wanker!' exclaimed Tony as he got into the car. 'A party that went wrong? What bloody planet is he on?'

'Have we really done a detailed study of the crime scene?' observed Simon.

'Enough. We'd find nothing there, not with your friend following us around. Besides, I found the information I wanted. In the stairwell. It was stuck to the wall. An advert for a coffee shop in Acton. The Haroun Al Rashid. When you get back from the butcher's, you can check it out.'

'You mean you want me to go there?'

'God, no. Just find out who owns it and how long it's been established.'

Simon asked Tony whether he fancied a liquid lunch, but Tony explained he was meeting Robert in Bloomsbury and that he would appreciate Simon giving him a lift to his flat so he could pick up his car.

'Will Robert want to know all about what has happened?'

'No,' replied Tony. 'Robert is very discreet.'

And they drove off, Tony to meet Robert, and Simon to renew his acquaintance with Bullock at the autopsy.

Chapter 3
A Meeting with Saleem Khan

Hassan Muglah in his one-room flat in Wapping watched the programme with disgust, as did Saleem Khan. But he watched it in the comfort of his very smart house in St John's Wood. Both men were watching a Sunday afternoon politics programme. It involved a Muslim cleric and Charles Richardson from the LGBT organisation. The cleric was making the point that according to the Quran, homosexuality is in the same chapter as the one in the Bible that relates to Sodom and Gomorrah. 'The act of same-sex indulgence is seen as a sin rather than a crime.'

The interviewer quickly asked a question. 'According to Sharia law?'

The cleric smiled. 'We live in a country where homosexuality is not against the law, but that does not mean to say that we do not consider it a sin. As does the Roman Catholic church, and large numbers of members of the Church of England.'

The interviewer then turned to Richardson to ask for his take on the cleric's statement. Richardson was a passionate speaker, and often went off-message when expressing his views.

'I understand you have an original slant on the murder of the gay men?' asked the interviewer.

Richardson was rather pompous and self-important. 'I wouldn't say original, more logical. If we look at the natural world, then nature takes care of its own.'

'Evolution,' was the interjection.

'Exactly,' continued Richardson. 'We live in an over-populated world, and to reduce the numerical crisis of too many mouths to feed and too few resources, Nature has put in a safety valve by increasing the number of gay people, who by their nature fail to procreate, and thus help to influence the swelling birth-rate. Society, therefore, should encourage young people who are, could be, or are on the cusp, to actively accept their homosexuality and promote gay sex as a means of solving one of Earth's major problems.'

'Nonsense,' cried the cleric. 'Absolute poppycock.'

'No more rubbish,' retaliated Richardson, 'than you quoting from Sodom and Gomorrah, no doubt a fictional story that's five thousand years old.'

'Ludicrous,' muttered the cleric.

'Is it?' Richardson smiled with a contemptuous and arrogant look. 'Could Mohammad not have been gay? And the question should be asked if Jesus Christ and his twelve male disciples…'

At this, the cleric stood up and started shouting, 'Blasphemy. Blasphemy! It is outrageous that you are able to express such opinions on national television.'

The interviewer, realising that the interview was getting out of control, could see headlines in tomorrow's papers suggesting that the BBC was condoning such opinions. He interjected sharply. 'I really think, Mr Richardson, you have gone too far. I would ask you to withdraw your comments.'

'On what grounds?' retorted Richardson.

'Of causing offence to many people of all faiths.'

Richardson, holding his hands up in mock surrender, and speaking with a smug sneer in his voice, 'I surrender! I surrender! I apologise for saying what I believe to be the truth. I realise, in the Islamic world, truth is a very rare commodity.'

That was enough for the interviewer, who brought the discussion to a very swift close. Hassan's eyes had narrowed as he watched it. Saleem switched off the television, muttering his annoyance at such a discussion being broadcast as his wife, Miriam, and his two daughters entered the room. Miriam was a strikingly beautiful woman, as were her daughters, Alicia aged twelve, and Rianna, aged fifteen.

'I've come to show you your beautiful daughter in the dress I made for her.'

Khan was still irritated by the television interview and only cursorily looked up. 'My daughters are always beautiful,' he said.

'But look at the dress. I bought the fabric and pattern in that little dress-shop in Hounslow, you remember,' continued Miriam.

Khan looked up and took notice. Rianna was wearing an Islamic-style dress and scarf, in a lightly brocaded white material. She looked quite stunning.

'Why is she wearing such a dress?'

'You know why,' exclaimed Miriam. 'For her school prom.'

Khan looked disdainful. He had accepted much of English culture, but this American-influenced prom was, in his view, a step too far.

'It is too good,' cried Khan. 'You'll have boys leering at you.'

'What, in a Catholic girls' school, with nuns overlooking the proceedings?'

'I don't like it,' muttered Khan.

Miriam looked despairing. 'Please don't let us have another argument. You agreed that Rianna could go, and that's an end of it.'

Khan knew that when Miriam signalled an end to it, that it was indeed the end, and there was no need to discuss the matter further. Any argument would have been cut short anyway by the chiming of the doorbell. Moments later, a young woman entered the room and informed the family that there was a man at the door requesting to meet with Saleem.

'What's his name?' asked Saleem.

'Tony Assad,' replied the girl.

Saleem's face lit up at once. 'Tony,' he cried. 'Show him in, Tia.' He turned to his wife. 'Fancy Tony calling. You remember him, don't you?'

'No,' replied Miriam. 'You have often spoken of him, but we have never met. Do you want us to leave?'

'No, no you and the girls must stay and meet Tony,' ordered Saleem. At this point, Tony was ushered into the room. 'Tony, my friend, how good to see you.'

'Salaam Alaikum,' was Tony's smiling response.

'Salaam, my friend,' continued Saleem. 'Let me introduce you to my daughters, Alicia and Rianna, and my beautiful wife Miriam.'

'Good to meet you, Miriam.' Tony looked puzzled. 'It's a very beautiful name.'

'For a very beautiful woman,' continued Saleem, not picking up on Tony's curiosity.

Miriam, however, was fully aware. She smiled at Tony and responded to his quizzical eye. 'I think your friend looks at me with curiosity, and asks the puzzling question, what is a woman with a Jewish-sounding name doing married to a Muslim cleric?'

Saleem now understood. 'Ah, I see. Even in the Muslim world, one follows the heart.'

'I'm not sure all Muslims would see it that way,' carped Tony.

Saleem smiled. 'There was much opposition, especially as the Jewish faith goes through the female line. Indeed, Miriam faced more antagonism than I did, some of her once-close friends refuse to acknowledge her even to this day. We are what you could call a multicultural family. I'm a Muslim, married to a Jewish woman, both daughters at a Catholic school, and my agnostic son at university. My children, if they wished, could take the Jewish faith. The girls haven't or are too young to make a decision. Rianna, indicating her clothes, likes dressing as a Muslim woman. Something of a fashion statement, but I'm not sure how much further it goes. My son likes mechanical engineering, parties, and young ladies.'

'And that's how it should be,' butted in Miriam, remembering their earlier conversation.

Saleem, remembering his manners, introduced Tony to the family. 'Miriam, you remember Tony, he was the agent who saved my life when I gave that talk in Hull.'

Miriam rebuked Tony, showing that she had not altogether forgotten her Jewish upbringing and Jewish humour. 'So it is you that I have to blame for him still being alive. I was hoping for a good insurance pay-out.'

'She is joking,' explained Saleem. Tony smiled.

'Would you like some mint tea?' enquired Saleem.

'Oh, no, thank you. I may be Moroccan, but mint tea I find is not to my taste. Too sweet.'

'I agree,' cried Saleem. 'Mint tea may be good in North Africa, but not here. Nice Indian tea in a proper English teapot? Yes?'

'That would be far more acceptable,' agreed Tony. Miriam and the girls immediately left the room to prepare a very English afternoon tea.

Once the ladies had gone, Saleem offered Tony a seat, reiterated how pleased he was to see him, and then asked directly why Tony had come. 'As much as it's good to see you, Tony, I cannot believe there is not a subtext to your visit.'

'You are right,' agreed Tony. 'Though it is good to see you looking so well, the main reason for my visit is to pick your brains, or maybe more to ask for advice.'

'You are welcome, my friend,' smiled Saleem.

As soon as Tony started accounting for the visit, Saleem became agitated and angry. 'I was watching a discussion on the television on this subject just before you came. It made me very angry.'

'In what way?' enquired Tony.

'It was a discussion,' explained Saleem, 'between a pompous Englishman and a Muslim cleric. The Englishman's view, though flawed, was to some extent logical. The cleric, on the other hand, rather than sitting passively and saying, that is your opinion but not mine, jumped up and started screaming blasphemy, and almost imposed a fatwah there and then. Such hysteria does nothing for Anglo-Muslim relationships.'

Tony agreed. He then explained that he was the MI5 operative looking into the rooftop atrocities.

Saleem nodded. 'The rooftop murders are copied from similar activities in Syria and Iraq. My brother, who is still in Syria, tells me of fathers who, suspecting their sons of unnatural behaviour, offer them to the city elders to be condemned.'

'I am to oversee British Intelligence's response to these deaths,' explained Tony.

Saleem was surprised. 'Deaths, not murders?' There was definite puzzlement in his voice.

'I do what I am told,' continued Tony. 'If you ask me personally, yes, murders. Cold-blooded murders.'

Saleem sat back in his chair, looking carefully at his guest. 'And how can I help?'

'I thought you may have some insight.'

Saleem remained still for a moment, summoning up his thoughts. 'Up to 2005,' he expounded, 'atrocities in this country could be laid at the feet of Mujajiroun. In 2005, as you must know, your government, in their wisdom, declared them a terrorist organisation and had them banned. To be a member of the Mujajiroun was illegal and to belong to it could and would leave you wide open to arrest as a terrorist. That does not mean to say the members of the Mujajiroun disappeared. They just went underground and formed new cells.'

'No major cell took Mujajiroun's place?'

Saleem rebuked Tony. 'You're MI5, you should know. I believe there are many smaller independent cells, more difficult to detect.'

Tony accepted this analysis, but he wanted to know the word on the street.

'Word on the street.' Saleem laughed. 'You make me sound like a New York gangster. I don't know the word on the street, as you put it, but I know the words used by my friends and the people I know. Anger, frustration, despair, gratitude, sadness. The list is endless.'

Tony picked upon one word. 'Frustration?'

'The Muslim community hope for a Muslim world with Muslim values,' continued Saleem. 'But I fear that will never come. They see pictures of young European girls in the 1900s, showing restraint in their dress and behaviour. They see them in the 1930s, still with restraint. Then they see photos of young girls today, loud, common, smoking, drinking, swearing, generally vulgar, and they think will our girls turn out this way in this heathen country? We must protect them. They feel there should be a strong moral code that young people should be bound by.'

'I am sure there are many British families who would agree with you.' Tony somehow resented Saleem taking such moral high ground. He knew of many Muslim youths who did not fit into the picture Saleem was trying to paint.

'No one does anything,' said Saleem with despair in his voice. 'These young men were put to death because of their sexual orientation. Many Muslims will agree, not with the means of death, but with the strict condemnation of what they see as things that are morally wrong.'

Tony interjected. 'But surely you don't?'

Saleem was indignant. 'Of course not. You ask me the word on the street. The people are wanting true moral values to be shown, true moral leadership. The Western world is weak and decadent. I believe in love, Tony, between a man and a woman, a man and a man, a woman and a woman, a Catholic and a Protestant, or a Jew and a Muslim.'

As if on cue, Miriam re-entered the room, followed by Tia with a large tray. 'English tea,' said Miriam proudly. 'In an English teapot. Also home-made baklava, and a home-made Victoria sponge. Just to show we don't discriminate between cultures in this house.'

Tony was humbled by Miriam's generosity.

Chapter 4
The Washing Machine

While Tony was being entertained in St John's Wood by the Khan family, Simon had the dubious pleasure of attending the post-mortem of the three dead men with Chief Inspector Bullock. It was a post-mortem unlike any Simon had attended before. The three bodies were laid out on three tables and a different pathologist was dealing with each body. The chief pathologist was co-ordinating the proceedings, making notes, and giving instructions.

'Julian couldn't stand the sight of all the blood, eh?' quipped Bullock, as they started work on the cadaver.

'His name's Tony,' responded Simon with a grim face.

Bullock continued, 'A right Julian Clary if you ask me.'

'How old are you?' snapped Simon.

'Why?' was Bullock's defiant response.

'Well, don't you think you should start acting your age?'

Bullock shrugged. 'Only joking, mate, only joking. He seemed a nice enough guy. But British Intelligence has always had its fair share of woofters. Ever since Burgess and Maclean.'

Simon looked at him with disgust. 'You amaze me,' he retorted, and turned his attention to the post-mortem which was being performed in front of them.

After three hours of cutting, sawing, weighing, and stitching, the chief examiner invited them into his office. Present were Bullock, Simon, and young Teddy Fisher, who had been eating jelly babies throughout the proceedings.

The examiner introduced himself as Dr Pearson and explained why he'd had all three post-mortems conducted at the same time. 'I wanted an immediate and direct comparison between the deaths, and I believe it was entirely the right decision. My report will take several days to compile, but I thought it important for you to have my immediate analysis.'

Bullock expressed his gratitude.

Pearson acknowledged this. 'Quite so,' he said. Then he cleared his throat and began to speak in a sober, meticulous manner. 'Let me make it clear from the start that these were not accidental deaths, but murders of a particularly grisly and sadistic nature.'

Simon looked at Bullock but got no reaction.

'All three deaths,' continued Dr Pearson, 'were the result of falling from a great height. Brain trauma was common to all, and all had broken spines. The interesting thing is that the deaths appeared to take place fifteen minutes apart. A risky procedure, but one for you to look into, not part of my remit. What is part of my remit is the time period before their deaths. Tox report states that there was a substantial amount of Rohypnol in their bloodstreams. The stomach contents were interesting. All three men had been fed exactly the same diet: couscous, chicken and assorted vegetables: mainly aubergines, peppers, onions and carrots.'

'Typical North African food,' muttered Bullock. 'They'd obviously been held captive.'

'Yes,' continued the doctor. 'Rope marks around their wrists and ankles would suggest they had been held against their will. Now we come to the grisly part. All three men had been castrated, but the most unpleasant bit is what happened to their anal passages.'

'They were all queer,' butted in Teddy, as he swallowed another jelly baby. 'We guessed they were gay from the message that Muslim fellow gave!'

Pearson was getting angry with the young detective's flippancy. 'What you didn't guess was the barbaric torture they had undergone. Not only had they been castrated without anaesthetic; they had also been penetrated by numerous objects, some of them sharp or serrated. Body number three looks as though he had been penetrated by a large kitchen knife. Their anal passages were butchered in a way more commonly seen in the Middle Ages.'

Simon was wondering how he was going to relate this to Tony, an openly gay man.

'There is worse to come,' continued the doctor.

Worse, thought Simon, *how could it possibly be worse?*

'Apart from intensely cruel sadism,' continued Pearson, 'acts of humiliation were meted out to the men. Their stomach contents contained copious amounts of urine. The men had either drunk, or been forced to drink, each other's urine.'

Simon felt sick. Even Bullock looked pale. Teddy, however, came out with a comment that seemed unbelievably crass.

'Well, that was kinky, wasn't it?'

The doctor turned on him. 'I've had to endure your lack of respect during this post-mortem as you gobbled your sweets,' he cried. 'But to make a comment like that after I have just given the agonising details of the most gruesome and torturous deaths, is beyond contempt. Please leave my office and wait in reception for your colleagues.'

Bullock should have stood up for his sergeant, who slunk out of the room, but he was still suffering from the traumatic details he had just heard and was having to digest. He said nothing.

Simon, on the other hand, wanted more details. 'You said that the third man had been penetrated by a large kitchen knife. Surely that would have resulted in much blood?'

'Certainly,' responded the doctor.

'But there was no blood,' Simon said puzzled. 'You also mentioned, Doctor, that all three men had been assaulted by objects. What other objects?'

'It's impossible for me to say,' explained the doctor, 'but if I were to make a guess, kitchen tools. Bottles, cheese graters, even, without sounding comical, a rolling pin.'

Bullock had now composed himself. 'And how long would you estimate these men had been held?'

'One had been a captive for a while. Maybe a week, maybe more. The other two not so long, a couple of days at the most. I am sorry I cannot be more helpful.'

And with that, the post-mortem was concluded.

***

Charles Richardson had a definite spring in his step as he left the insurance offices at which he worked. He was pleased with the way his interview on the television had gone the night before. It seemed to have impressed most of his colleagues, though some of the young girls in the office thought his outburst rather funny. Not the reaction he expected, but better than negativity.

It was only a ten-minute walk from his office to the flat he had lived in for the last forty years, first with his mother, then alone since her death in 1998. He stopped at the local news agent's to buy an evening paper, looking for a report of his interview. *I'll read that after tea*, he thought. He arrived at Kingswood Court and took the lift up to number twelve on the fourth floor. He admired his clean front door. Once a week he wiped the door with a damp cloth. Mr Richardson was fastidious, as could be seen by the interior of the flat. Spotlessly clean and everything in its place. He was, he guessed, a little OCD, but he was rather proud of that. Better be obsessively tidy and clean than a slob. He went into the lounge, stopped, and looked with amazement, not at the photo of his mum or the fact that a couple of flowers in a vase had started to wilt. No, what Richardson was staring at was a large box.

'What on earth!' he exclaimed and marched directly out of the flat and rang the doorbell of number eleven opposite. Mrs Rhodes opened the door.

'Hello, Mr Richardson,' she smiled. 'And how are you today? I've got a friend around for a cup of tea. We were discussing seeing you on the telly last night.'

Charles was not interested. 'There is a large box in my flat,' he explained. 'Do you know anything about it?'

'It's your new washing machine. It was delivered about half an hour ago.'

'I haven't ordered a washing machine,' exploded Charles.

'Well, the man who delivered it said it was for your address. I wouldn't have let him in otherwise. You'd better ring Riley's, the electrical shop on the High Street. I believe that's where it came from.'

'Yes, I will,' stammered Charles. 'And, er, thank you,' he added begrudgingly.

'They're always getting orders wrong,' continued Mrs Rhodes. 'I blame the internet. Not like it used to be when I was a girl.'

Charles didn't care about that. He turned on his heel and returned to his flat with the sole purpose of phoning Riley's and giving them a piece of his mind. But he was examining the box to see if there were any delivery details when suddenly he heard a noise in the kitchen.

Mr Snowball was sitting on the work surface. Mr Snowball was a large white Persian cat. Charles's OCD kicked in. 'Mr Snowball, get down, you know you're not supposed to be on kitchen surfaces. Now I'll have to give it a good clean.'

The cat meowed.

'Oh, very well, Mr Snowball. I know you want your evening meal, but so do I.'

Charles picked up the cat's bowl and squeezed a sachet of cat food into it. He had a ritual: feed the cat, then change the litter tray, a job he really disliked. And then tonight the extra task of cleaning the work surface. All these tasks took his mind off the box in the lounge, and he was quite surprised when the doorbell rang.

'Who on earth can that be?' he muttered to himself. Cleaning his hands, he went to the front door and opened it.

Facing him was a man in overalls and a baseball cap, and with a sack barrow.

'Yes?' Charles said impatiently.

'I made a mistake with my order,' replied the man. 'I only just realised it when I looked at my order book. The washing machine I delivered was not for this address. I thought it was for 12 Kingswood Court, and it's not, you see, it's for 12 Kingswood Close, just around the corner.'

Charles hated his structured life to be disrupted, but he had to accept the situation, particularly if he wanted rid of the box.

'Well, you'd better come in,' he ordered, and led the man down the hall to the lounge. He turned to speak to the man, and that was the last he remembered. Hassan Muglah fired the taser straight at him. Charles fell, and Hassan swiftly injected him with a drug to knock him out. He then pushed Charles into the box. Inserting the sack barrow under the box, he wheeled it away.

Mrs Rhodes was saying goodbye to her friend as Hassan wheeled the large box out. 'Oh, you've come to collect it. That was quick.'

'Yes,' said Hassan. 'I realised I'd got the wrong address when I consulted my order book.'

Mrs Rhodes turned to her friend to explain what had happened and to wish her good night. 'I don't want to push you away, luv, but it's Claudia and Tess on the One Show, discussing strictly, and I don't wish to miss it.'

By this time Hassan was in the lift. He pressed the button for the ground floor, and Hassan, Charles, and the washing machine box disappeared.

Chapter 5
A Visit to North Yorkshire

The A1 is one of the most boring roads, thought Tony, *but it is the most direct way to get to Pickering.* To pass the time, he put on the radio. He was listening to a conservation programme about protecting eels in the mouth of the Thames. It was not the sort of programme he usually chose to listen to, but it whiled away the journey, and he actually became quite interested in what he found to be a threatened species. He stopped for a coffee at a service station somewhere in the Lincoln/Nottingham area, then continued the rest of the journey listening to John Denver and Johnny Cash. He loved *A Boy Named Sue* and thought the simple story had so much resonance in today's society. Beyond York, he turned off the A1, and headed towards Scarborough. He drove to Pickering, and from there he took the A169 to Dalby Forest. Miranda, his mother, lived in a large Georgian farmhouse, very grand, but very isolated. Too isolated, Tony thought, but his mother liked the solitude, and was well protected by Mr Dick and Trotwood, two beautiful but aggressive Rhodesian Ridgeback dogs. They were given Dickensian names because his mother loved Dickens. She also had a cat called Mr Micawber. Tony drove up to the house and was greeted by two barking dogs. He remained in the car until his mother called them to heel.

'You'll be okay now,' cried his mother.

Tony wasn't so sure. Mr Dick was growling and looked very threatening. His mother, sensing Tony's discomfort, told him she'd take the dogs into the back garden and lock them out. Miranda was a tall, dignified woman. She wore jeans and a sweater and, though casual in her dress, could never be described as scruffy. For a woman approaching 70, she was remarkably youthful in her looks. After ushering the dogs out, she was able to greet her son properly. 'Darling, it's lovely to see you. Is it a social call or business?'

Tony looked sheepish.

'Never mind, you'll have to join me in the lab.' This was the term she used for her kitchen. 'I'm working on a new programme, cooking tripe and pigs' trotters. Old Graham Kerr recipe.'

'It looks and smells disgusting,' declared Tony.

'Tunisian tripe dish. Basically, it's tripe, pickled trotters, carrots, tomatoes, peppers, onions, a leek, and two cloves of garlic. Try some,' offered his mother.

'I'd rather die,' said Tony, 'and after looking at that I've no doubt I would.'

'I'll make a coffee and we'll have it in the lounge,' decided his mother. 'I can then check Mr Dick isn't digging up any of my winter bulbs.'

Tony went into a beautifully furnished Georgian lounge filled with priceless antiques, from an inlaid Sheraton desk and Hepplewhite chairs, to a collection of blue and white Chinese vases from the Kang Hsi and Chien Lung periods. It was not long before his mother entered with a tray on which was a pot of percolated coffee and two china mugs with a matching milk jug and sugar bowl.

Miranda sat near the French windows so that she could keep her eye on Mr Dick. 'So what brings you to North Yorkshire, if it's not for pleasure?' she asked.

Tony again looked ashamed.

'Pity it's not for pleasure,' continued his mother. 'Walks through the forest at this time of year can be very invigorating.'

'I'm sure they can,' responded Tony.

'Well, what's troubling the North African desk?' enquired his mother. 'What brings you 300 miles to see your dear old mother?'

'That's a bit of an exaggeration,' corrected Tony.

'What is?' asked Miranda.

'That it's 300 miles.'

'Well, tell Mummy the problem.'

Tony smiled. 'You've no doubt read about the murder of three gay men, thrown to their deaths from a rooftop in London?'

'Sad,' responded Miranda, in a matter-of-fact manner. 'A direct copy of the punishment ladled out in Homs in Syria by ISIS.' Miranda paused, thought a little, and continued. 'What I found most disturbing about the Homs atrocity were the crowds in the street watching. Some of them were children who had been brought by their parents to watch the gruesome execution. It was as though we'd gone back to the Middle Ages.'

'There were no crowds in London,' commented Tony.

'Did it upset Alan?' enquired Miranda.

'Mother,' cried Tony in exasperation. 'Alan and I parted over six years ago. I live with Robert, a solicitor.'

'Oh, yes, of course,' smiled Miranda. 'Tall, handsome man, looks as though he is well-endowed.'

'Mother, please,' exploded Tony.

Miranda loved teasing her son, and Tony hated it when his mother talked so openly about sexual and private matters.

'Do you plan to settle down with him on a more permanent basis?' asked Miranda, trying to pacify her offended son.

'We've lived together for five years, so maybe,' explained Tony.

'Well,' enquired Miranda. 'How can I help you with the rooftop murders?'

'You remember the burning of that priest last year?' asked Tony.

'Yes,' mused Miranda. 'In a field not far from here. A most unsatisfactory conclusion.'

Tony was puzzled. 'In what way unsatisfactory? Three men are about to stand trial for the crime.'

Miranda answered his question with her usual directness. 'Yes, they are about to stand trial, and will undoubtedly get heavy custodial sentences, but the leader got away, and it was not just that which bothered me. It was the singularity of the act. The aim of these jihadists, from what I understand, is to strike fear and terror into our placid Christian society. Well, it certainly shocked, but it was never followed up.'

'Exactly,' agreed Tony. 'Behind the burning was the same motive that lay behind these recent executions.'

'So you think the killings are linked?'

'Could be.'

Miranda sat still for a moment, deep in memories. Then she laughed. 'The leader of the group was David Green.'

'Hardly an Islamic name,' commented Tony. 'And what's so amusing?'

'The reason I remember the name,' said Miranda, with a wicked twinkle in her eye, 'was because there was a man at MI5 when I first worked there called David Green. Now, he was a big boy.'

Tony reprimanded her. 'Mother, I don't wish to know.'

'He was big, six foot three, and as broad as Hercules.'

Tony glowered at her.

'But back to the David you're interested in. His father married a girl from Libya. David renounced his Christian name and took another, Haroun Al Rashid.'

Tony laughed. 'That's not real. It sounds like a name out of the Arabian Nights.'

Miranda continued. 'David was a bright boy. Went to Leeds grammar school, then to Nottingham uni, where he took a joint degree in economics and politics. It was while he was at university that he was radicalised. He worked in Brentford, London, at a branch of Barclays. While he was presenting to the world an upright and conservative figure of the establishment, he was working out his Islamic strategy.'

Tony marvelled at his mother's depth of knowledge, and then asked the pertinent question. 'What was his strategy?'

'He wanted to stop the flow of young people to Syria and Iraq and encourage them to fight the West within Europe. He wanted to destabilise the complacent attitude of the western European public by committing violent and horrific acts of terrorism under the guise of Sharia law. He wanted to strike at the centre of our moral codes, challenging what he believes is right and what is wrong in today's western society.'

Tony looked puzzled. 'Mother, how the hell do you know all this, and how in God's name do you remember it?'

She smiled. 'After the sacrificial burning you were busy in Hull, if you remember, so Mark phoned me and asked if I would prepare a detailed report on the incident. But surely you've seen it?'

'Never,' said Tony crossly. 'I didn't even know it existed.'

'Now why does that not surprise me?' remarked Miranda. 'And why do I remember the details so clearly? Mark rang me to say that you were coming down to discuss the incident, so I thought I'd read through my report. I printed a copy for you.'

Tony took it from her graciously, though still irritated, not with his mother, but with Mark's high-handedness.

Miranda looked at her watch. 'My goodness, it's 4:30 pm. I know you'd planned to return to London today, but it's a long journey, and I don't see you often. Why don't you stay the night?'

Tony didn't take much persuading. Driving back down the A1 was not something he relished.

Miranda spoke. 'I have an idea. Just outside Thirsk is Tommy Banks' restaurant. His food is delicious and quite unique. Why don't I book a table there?'

Tony quickly agreed. Anything would be better than the concoction his mother had been preparing. While Tony read the report compiled by his mother, Miranda rang the restaurant to book a table, but was told it was fully booked. When she said she was Miranda Assad, they miraculously found a table and booked it for 8 pm. The Black Swan at Oldstead was a delightful country pub, way off the beaten track. It seemed incredible to Tony that in such a remote and rural area he was able to sit down to a 12-course tasting menu containing such things as walnut tart, sour bread and sour butter, scallops with spruce potatoes and fermented celeriac, and eight more courses which sounded weird but tasted delicious.

'To think,' said Tony, 'that I live in the centre of London where there are restaurants on every corner, but I have to come out to the wilds of North Yorkshire to taste food that is quite wonderful and certainly original.'

Miranda smiled, content to have a rare meal with her son. Nothing was said about the case until they got home at about 12:30 am. Miranda was reunited with her beloved dogs. Mr Dick was licking Tony's face while Trotwood was trying to stick her nose between his legs. 'Why do they do that?' Tony asked.

'Scent, she wants to recognise your scent.'

The dogs eventually settled down, and over the requisite glass of Scotch that Miranda drank every night before retiring, Tony brought up the question of motive. 'Why burn the priest?' he asked.

Miranda explained that the quiet priest had been quite vocal when it came to women's rights. 'Though he objected to women bishops in the Church of England, he was quite outspoken when it came to his views on the attitude of men towards women in the Muslim faith. He called it not only offensive in this day and age, but an abomination against God himself. He then went on to call Muhammad a misogynist.'

Tony whistled. 'That's strong stuff. A fatwah on him would, therefore, have been inevitable.'

'Absolutely,' said Miranda, as she poured another whisky into Tony's glass.

'No more,' cried Tony. 'I've got an early start tomorrow.' He was about to retire for the evening, when curiosity got the better of him. 'This David Green who worked at MI5?'

'Oh, it was a long time before I met your father,' explained Miranda.

'And what was his job at MI5?'

'He was the janitor,' smiled Miranda. 'In those days I liked a bit of rough.'

'Mother, that's going too far!' exclaimed Tony and retired to his bedroom with the glass of Scotch, thinking what a hypocrite he was. Many a bit of rough had shared his bed.

At 9 the following morning, Miranda woke him with a cup of tea and told him there would be breakfast for him downstairs.

'Luxury,' smiled Tony, and having drunk the tea, he jumped in the shower and did his usual toilet. He smiled. His mother had laid out a razor, realising he hadn't brought one with him.

Downstairs, he faced a large English breakfast of bacon, two eggs, three sausages, mushrooms and fried bread, but no hash browns. The latter were fine in McDonald's, but not in the home of Miranda Assad. There was also a large pot of steaming coffee.

'I thought you said a small breakfast,' complained Tony. 'I'm used to a slice of toast and a coffee.'

'I wanted to feed you up before your long journey back to that hateful city.' Miranda laughed as she placed toast and home-made marmalade on the table.

At ten-thirty, and feeling extraordinarily full, Tony kissed his mother and left for 'that dreadful city', as Miranda called London.

The journey back always seemed shorter than the journey there, and Tony couldn't really understand why. About midday his phone rang. Luckily, he was on hands-free, so was able to talk.

'Where the hell are you?' yelled Mark.

'You know where I am,' responded Tony in an angry voice. 'I've been at my mother's, as you are only too well aware.'

'Oh yes,' replied Mark, in a somewhat humble voice. He then returned to his usual direct manner. 'There's been another incident. A man called Charles Richardson has been found crucified with his cock cut off and stuffed down his throat. I've sent Newlove to the scene, but I want you to take over as soon as you get back.'

The phone went dead, and palpable concern ran through Tony's body. 'What the hell is going on?' he cried to himself.

Chapter 6

An Irrational Conversation

By the time Simon arrived, the forensic team had pulled the nails out of Charles Richardson's hands and were taking him out to the waiting ambulance. Bullock was there, looking intensely concerned, while Teddy was amusing himself looking through artwork stacked in a corner of the lock-up.

'They say his chances of survival are slim,' remarked Bullock, as Simon entered. 'In all my years in the Met, I have never seen anything like it.'

'Who is he?' enquired Simon.

'According to the contents of his wallet,' reported Bullock, 'he's a Charles Richardson of 12 Kingswood Court, Acton.'

Bullock turned to Teddy with a degree of irritation. 'Teddy, what the hell are you doing?'

'Looking, just looking,' replied Teddy. 'There are some fine pieces of work here.'

Bullock dismissed his comments as irrelevant. 'Get yourself down to the Middlesex Hospital and sit at Richardson's bedside until he comes around, if he ever does,' he instructed. 'If he does come around, call me.'

'Who found him?' asked Simon.

'The young woman who rents the lock-up as a studio,' explained Bullock. 'A Miss Charlie Briggs. She's sitting outside. She's a bit shaken up.'

'Who wouldn't be?' responded Simon grimly.

Simon and Bullock went outside to have a chat with Charlie Briggs.

'Miss Briggs,' said Bullock, 'I'm Chief Inspector Bullock, the senior investigating officer on this case, and this is Simon Newlove from MI5. A very nasty incident to witness. Now, I understand you were the first person on the scene?'

Both Bullock and Newlove were somewhat taken aback by the abrasive reaction from Miss Briggs. 'Very nasty incident? That's a nice way of putting it.'

'It must have been quite a shock,' continued Bullock.

'No,' replied Charlie scornfully. 'I see crucified men every day of the week. Of course it was a shock. I don't think I'll ever get over it.'

Simon decided it was time to intervene. 'Would you mind going over exactly what happened?'

To begin with, she seemed irritated at having to retell what had happened. 'I arrived on my bike, at about 8.30 am.' She was beginning to calm down as she narrated the story. 'I cycled up to the lock-up which I use as an upholstery workshop, unlocked the door, and opened it. Brought my bike into the room, then switched on the light. It's a dark space and my eyes took time to adjust. Then I saw him. Against the wall, blood pouring from between his legs. It was terrible, worse than terrible, horrific.' Charlie lost her composure and started to cry.

'Have you anyone who can be with you?' asked Simon.

'I've phoned my mother; she's coming to collect me.'

'I don't want to be insensitive,' interrupted Bullock, 'but have you any idea how someone could have got into your workshop?'

A definite no from Charlie.

'What about keys?' insisted Bullock.

'I understand from the letting agency,' replied Charlie, 'that I have the only keys. Apart from the ones the agency keeps for security reasons.'

'We'll need the name of the letting agency,' explained Simon.

'Of course. It's Peacock's in the High Street. Mrs Brighton looks after my let.'

'Have you loaned your key to anyone?' persisted Bullock.

'No, definitely not,' came the reply.

'Anything unusual about the key?' continued Bullock.

Charlie looked puzzled. 'What do you mean?'

'Well,' began Bullock. 'Had it been lost recently? Have you found it in a place you wouldn't expect?'

'Now you come to mention it, yes.' Charlie started to give an explanation. 'I take an evening class in upholstery every Tuesday at Hammersmith College. About two weeks ago, Peter, one of my students, said to me, "Is this your key, Charlie?" It was lying on the bench near all the modelling stuff. I couldn't understand why it should be there. I normally keep it in my bag. Why would it be on a bench in the school where I take a night class? It didn't make sense.'

'Peter?' asked Bullock kindly.

'Yes,' replied Charlie. 'Peter Grainger.'

'Address?' asked Bullock.

'It'll be at my flat, in my college folder,' she replied.

47

'We'll need all your students' addresses,' instructed Bullock.

'Of course,' replied Charlie. 'Though you'll have to go to the College administration for most of them.'

A cup of tea had arrived for Charlie, which she willingly accepted, and the two men left the grisly scene.

***

On his journey back from Pickering, Tony had decided that Simon was more than competent to examine the crime scene, leaving Tony free to visit the Haroun Al Rashid coffee shop in Acton. First, however, he went home and put on his gallabiyah and kufi. He looked at himself in the long mirror and admired his authentic Muslim look.

On entering the cafe, he observed that there were only a few tables free, and the clientele was exclusively male. He went up to the counter, and after the usual salaams, ordered a herbal tea. He spoke to the man behind the bar in Arabic to establish his North African credentials, then went to sit near the window at one of the few free tables. He hadn't been there more than five minutes before he was addressed by a tall, dark, bearded man, also dressed in a gallabiyah, and saying, 'Salaam Alaikum.'

'Salaam,' replied Tony.

'Do you mind if I join you at your table?' asked the man. 'All the other tables are taken.'

Tony noticed that this was not actually true; there were a couple of empty tables. However, he was only too pleased to have someone to talk to, and whom he hoped to pump for information about the place.

'You've been here a while?' asked the man.

'No, no just arrived,' was Tony's response.

'English?' enquired the man.

'No, Moroccan,' was the reply.

'You speak very good English,' smiled the man.

'Too good,' continued Tony. 'Went to school in Marrakesh.' He was beginning to wonder who was pumping whom.

'Marrakesh,' mused the man. 'I would love to go to Marrakesh.' He thought for a moment. 'Coming from that city, I am surprised you don't speak French.'

'I do speak French,' answered Tony, 'but my mother's English, married to a Moroccan teacher.'

'I'm mixed raced also,' responded the man, with a big smile on his face, 'but the other way around. My mother is Syrian, and my father is English.'

There was a silence, then suddenly the stranger asked a somewhat surprising question. He looked around, leaned forward, and, speaking in an almost conspiratorial voice, asked if Tony had come to see the brothers.

'Brothers?' Tony looked puzzled.

'Those men, over there, at that table,' explained the stranger. Tony looked over at a table where three men were sitting, two with long grey beards, and one with a thin black chinstrap beard.

The man continued, 'The brothers sit at that table after prayers every Friday, and one can put proposals forward to them.'

'Proposals?' asked Tony, beginning to feel excited. 'What sort of proposals?'

'Things to do with the Muslim community, and how to help people adjust to their adopted country,' replied Tony's new friend, with a suspicious look in his eye.

'Ah, right,' was Tony's response. He was rather disappointed with the answer he had been given. He had been hoping for a more sinister reply. 'That's very good,' he continued. 'I thought maybe…'

The man cut him short. 'That too. They listen, but don't act upon what is said.'

'Why?' asked Tony.

'I think they feel that it is good for people to express their radical views to help to relieve their inner tensions. There are many angry young men in our community, as I am sure you know.' The response was almost given as a rebuke. Tony felt that if that was all the brothers were doing, then all credit to them. He smiled at his new friend.

'So, they listen to radical views, but do nothing. They're acting rather like a safety valve.' He decided that this was not getting anywhere; he needed to find out more. 'How do you know they don't act on ideas?'

The stranger laughed. 'I like you.'

'Thanks.'

'Can I be honest with you? Can I, as a brother, trust you?'

'Of course.' Worrying over what was coming next.

'One time I took an idea to them,' declared the man.

'Really?' Tony became interested but was not prepared for what was to come.

'Pork,' said the man.

'Pork?' reiterated Tony.

'Pork,' continued the man. 'Muslims don't eat pork, do they, so if we were to infect the pork food chain, it would have a devastating effect on the West, without affecting Muslims.'

'And Jews,' smiled Tony.

'They could be dealt with later.'

'The final solution, eh?' Tony was beginning to think he was sitting with a paranoid schizophrenic.

'Are you mocking me?' cried his new-found friend.

'No, not at all. I was just wondering how you planned to infect the food chain.'

'Infect the animals' food with some form of chemically constructed virus.' He smiled as though it was a simple task, and Tony's question was naïve.

'But surely that would kill the pig before it killed the man?' Tony decided he was wasting his time talking to this man, but felt he had to push it a little further.

'And what did the brothers say when you presented your idea?'

'They understood,' said the man grudgingly. 'But told me the idea lacked clarity.'

Lacked clarity! Now that was the understatement of the day, thought Tony. 'You need their support?' he enquired.

'Of course. They have the money.'

'Ah, now I understand.' There was a pause, then Tony decided to take the bull by the horns. 'What about the rooftop killings?'

'What about them?' The man was becoming distracted.

'Well, did they get sanctioned by the brothers?'

'No, nothing was said about it. It's a group acting on their own. The brothers were not best pleased.'

'I could imagine,' agreed Tony. 'Had their noses pushed out of joint.'

'What do you mean by that?' challenged the man.

'Just an expression,' replied Tony defensively.

The man was becoming slightly belligerent. 'You ask many questions, my friend. I begin to wonder why.'

'I like you,' explained Tony amicably. 'You came and sat at my table. You asked me where I came from, you made me feel relaxed and welcome, and I enjoyed your observations.'

The man seemed happy with Tony's response, but Tony was not sure about this man. Why had he come to Tony's table, and why had he divulged such a ridiculous plan at a first meeting?

The man looked puzzled when Tony stood up.

'I must go,' explained Tony. 'Are you here every Friday?'

'Yes, every Friday. Have you plans?'

'Yes, I'm taking my niece to the zoo. Salaam, my friend.'

'Salaam,' was the stranger's response, as Tony hurried out of the bar, wondering what he had actually learnt.

As he sat in his car, he wondered why the man had not asked his name and why he hadn't asked the other's name. He smiled, because he knew they would both have lied.

Chapter 7
Things Start to Unravel

Everyone was collected together in the conference room at MI5. Tony was leading the meeting, which included Simon Newlove, Mark Selby, Felicity Morgan, Roger Johnson, Mike Bailey and Valerie Anderson.

'Four victims,' Tony started. 'Three dead and one critically ill. I think we must all agree that the four are connected and that there is one particularly nasty cell, which we have not picked up on, trying to intimidate the UK public.'

'Are we sure it's a cell?' asked Simon.

'Meaning?' responded Tony.

'Could it not be the act of an individual?'

'You've made a good point there,' agreed Tony. 'It could be the work of just one man. Do we know anything else?'

'Richardson,' began Felicity, 'though a member of the LGBT, was also a member of a fringe group called GNO – Gay Natural Order – encouraging people to accept their gay selves in order to reduce population size.'

'Crank,' muttered Mike Bailey.

'Not necessarily,' defended Felicity. 'He had been on the television the previous day and had made quite a vitriolic attack on the Muslim and Christian faiths, suggesting that both Christ and Muhammad were gay.'

'Well, that's definitely a motive,' commented Tony.

Felicity continued. 'On the day of his abduction, according to Richardson's neighbour, he received a washing machine in a large crate. Richardson was somewhat put out as he had not ordered a washing machine and was going to call the store. An hour later the neighbour saw a delivery man removing the machine, saying he had the wrong address.'

'Could she describe the man?' asked Tony.

'Tall, dark hair, dark skin, could be of Arabic descent. Oh, and he wore a baseball cap.'

'At least we know how he moved the body,' remarked Tony, and then turned to Roger Johnson. 'What about the three that were murdered?'

Johnson looked at his notes. 'Aaron Bakha, David Wheeler and Timothy Crawford.'

'How do we know this?' enquired Tony.

'They were all friends,' replied Johnson. 'David and Timothy had a civil partnership ceremony a couple of weeks ago, and Aaron, along with some other guy, were their witnesses. The Met found the certificate in David Wheeler's inside pocket.'

Tony looked puzzled. 'Either the assailant wasn't fully aware of Shariah law, or this wasn't an execution at all.'

'How do you make that out?' butted in Mark, making his first contribution.

According to Muslim law, though they don't agree with homosexuality, it is the one who takes on the role of the woman, the passive partner, who is the person that has committed the real sin.'

'Oh, the bitch.' Mike Bailey laughed.

Tony looked at him with disdain. 'I didn't know we had recruited Sergeant Teddy from the Met,' was Tony's sardonic comment.

'Who the hell's Sergeant Teddy?' griped Mark.

'A nobody, sir, a silly homophobic copper, who should have stayed in uniform.'

'Can we keep to the matter under discussion. Are you suggesting that the murder of these three men was not an act of terrorism?'

'All I know is that if two of the men were in a partnership, then according to Shariah law, only the passive partner should have been sacrificed. The other may have been beaten but freed.'

'Yes,' added Simon, 'but you know as well as I do that relationships vary. They could have both been versatile.'

'That's true,' agreed Tony. 'But how did the assailant know? To me, it looks like a very nasty sex crime covered with the veil of Islam. The perpetrator penetrated all three men for his own gratification. And there was the use of urine. Golden showers are not uncommon in the gay world.'

'Are you saying that the act was committed by a serial killer of gays, not a jihadist?'

'Yes,' continued Tony. 'Someone who feels guilty about his own sexuality. The guilt being reinforced if our killer was brought up in a strict Muslim family.'

'Do we then discount any connection between the murders of the men and that of Richardson?' asked Mark.

'Not at all,' commented Tony. 'The MO is different, but the intent is the same. The three men were murdered, but

Richardson was definitely the object of an attempted execution.'

'No longer attempted,' added Felicity. 'We've just had word from the Middlesex Hospital that Richardson has died from the wounds inflicted.'

The room went silent for a while, and then Tony continued. 'He was crucified, a Christian symbol. His penis was forced down his throat, suggesting he spoke out too much, as he obviously did when he offended Islam on television. All killings perpetrated by the same man, but some were sexual, and one a dramatic and cruel execution.'

'I think you could be right,' commented Mark. 'A Muslim psychopath who hates himself, or at least hates what he's become.'

'If the murder of the three guys was a straightforward hate crime, should we not simply hand it over to the Met?' asked Tony.

'No,' said Mark defiantly. 'Give the Met our thoughts on the killings, but I want you to stick with it until the man is caught. After all, your idea is only a theory, and it still could be a terrorist act.'

The group dispersed, but not before Mark called Tony into his office. 'You see I was right,' declared Mark, with a smug look on his face.

'Sir?' enquired Tony.

'Getting a queer Arab to lead the team. Who else had the knowledge to come up with such an idea?'

Tony looked at Mark with a look of confused resignation.

***

Robert and Tony were not aware they were being watched as they tucked into the Caesar salad in their favourite café in Bloomsbury. The man's binoculars never moved from them. He was watching them while feeling a stirring in his groin that he hated.

'I don't know whether it's more creepy,' moaned Robert, 'thinking he is a serial killer or wondering if he is a jihadist.'

'We'll have to be vigilant with our security,' emphasised Tony.

'You don't think he'd come after us!' exclaimed Robert, going visibly pale.

'If he finds out one of the team searching for him is gay, then there is a possibility,' mocked Tony. 'Don't worry, I'll have a couple of butch security guards outside our door to protect us, and when the guards get bored, they can always pop in for a cup of my China tea.'

'It's not a laughing matter,' continued Robert.

'I'm not laughing,' promised Tony. 'But there's no point in worrying about something that hasn't happened.'

Why don't we go and visit your mother in the New Forest?' suggested Robert.

'It's Dalby forest, near Scarborough. It's all hiking and orienteering. You'd hate it.'

'Your mother seems to like it,' persisted Robert.

'My mother is a batty recluse.'

Robert poured himself another cup of tea and asked Tony if he wanted a refill. 'No, I must away.'

'Where to this time?' enquired Robert.

'LSE, the London School of Economics.'

'I know what the LSE is,' rebuked Robert. 'What are you doing there?'

'Looking into the world of Adam Smith,' came Tony's sarcastic reply.

Robert resented it when Tony took him for a fool. 'I doubt it,' Robert replied. 'He's been dead for 200 years. Tony was getting up and moving to the door when Robert reminded him not to be late as he was cooking a lobster and crab pasta, and then they were to visit a new exhibition at the Tate Modern of art from the Bauhaus in the 1920s. Tony promised he wouldn't be late, and said that he was looking forward to the meal. He wasn't, however, so sure about the art exhibition. German surrealism didn't really rock his boat.

Tony left the café and the binoculars were put away.

Chapter 8
Questions and Answers

Simon was at the Hammersmith College of Further Education, asking Peter Grainger about the missing key. Peter was a fresh-faced man in his late twenties. He was laid-back and, though casual in his attitude, was quite willing to help the authorities in solving the gruesome crime.

'I found the key over here on the craft table,' said Peter. He took Simon to the table, which held paintbrushes, a Stanley knife, a basket of miscellaneous fabrics and a large ball of Plasticine.

'How did you know it was Charlie's key?' asked Simon.

'I didn't,' replied Peter. 'It had a tag on it that said lock-up, so I assumed it was hers.'

'Was it wet?' asked Simon.

'No. Why would it have been wet?'

'There's been quite a bit of rain recently. Someone may have taken it outside the college.'

'No. Though I do remember one thing. It was greasy,' responded Peter. 'I remember this because I made some lewd comment about lube having burst in her bag.' Peter noticed that Simon had been modelling with the Plasticine. 'That's good,' he observed. 'You should join the class.'

Simon smiled. 'It takes me back to my childhood. Very therapeutic. Is Plasticine always on the bench?'

'Always,' replied Peter.

'So it wouldn't be difficult for someone to make an impression of the key?'

'No, I suppose not,' agreed Peter.

Simon puzzled for a moment. 'Do you have any North African students on your course?'

'Not this year,' responded Peter.

'What about staff?'

'No,' replied Peter. His face suddenly lit up. 'We did have a technician working with us for a couple of weeks.' He tried to recall the name. 'Ali something or other. We used to call him Ali Baba.'

'I'm sure that went down well,' commented Simon sarcastically.

'Not very PC,' responded Peter, looking rather shame-faced. 'I think his real name was Hassan.'

***

While Simon was at the college of further education, Tony was in the upper echelons of the LSE. He had been directed to a lecture theatre where Doctor Bradbury had just finished giving a lecture. Bradbury was very aware of his academic status and spoke down to people as though they were some lower species of mankind. He wore a well-cut tweed suit and a pink bow tie, which added to the aesthetic and somewhat effeminate way he presented himself. Tony decided he didn't really care for him. He warily approached the learned doctor, who was speaking to a female student. Seeing that the doctor had almost finished, Tony cleared his throat and addressed him. 'Excuse me,' he interrupted. 'Are you by any chance Dr Bradbury?'

'Not by any chance,' replied Bradbury, in a superior voice. 'I am Dr Bradbury.' He turned to his student. 'I'm sorry, Caroline, we'll have to discuss the comments I made on your essay at a later date. This gentleman has obviously claimed priority.'

Tony ignored Bradbury's affront and asked him directly whether or not he was Aaron Bakha's tutor.

'I am indeed,' said Bradbury. 'And you are?'

Ignoring Bradbury's rudeness, Tony showed him his warrant card. Bradbury took it in a supercilious manner.

'Tony Assad, MI5,' he read. 'Am I supposed to be impressed?'

'Not unless you want to be,' replied Tony, who at that moment wished to punch Bradbury in the face. 'When did you last see Aaron?'

'Mr Assad, I don't keep a record of when I see all my students.' Bradbury, realising he had been rather rude even for him, stopped and recalled the moment. 'About a week ago. His essay on economic strategies in the late nineteenth century was late.' He returned to his usual pompous demeanour. 'Well, what's he been up to?'

'I'm afraid to inform you that Aaron is dead, murdered.'

If Bradbury was shocked, he didn't show it. 'Oh, that's sad. So young,' he replied. 'But I can't say I'm surprised.'

Tony was curious. 'Why are you not surprised, Dr Bradbury?'

'Lifestyle. Pretty lad, always had money. I could see why he was in demand. If you know what I mean?'

Tony was beginning to understand.

Bradbury went on. 'We're not to get involved with students. It would be inappropriate. But I used to tell him to be careful as there are a lot of bad men out there.'

Was Bradbury really showing compassion? Surely not. 'Do you know where he used to go?'

'The Blue Lagoon, Sloane Square. It's a sauna. Not very blue and not much of a lagoon. Rather sleazy, if you ask me. But Aaron seemed to like it.'

Tony relished the opportunity to follow this up. He smiled. 'Oh, so you've been there?'

Bradbury was obviously embarrassed as he realised what he had said. 'I went once with Aaron, as his guest. He wanted to show me what he called his hunting-ground. Not my sort of place.'

'Did he mention anyone he knew there, any friends?' continued Tony.

'A lad called Terry,' replied Bradbury, then hastily added, 'Don't know him. Never met him. But I know that Aaron and he were good friends.' He resumed his usual contemptuous manner. 'They used to offer a ménage-à-trois, I believe.'

'Oh, very pally.' Tony turned again to Bradbury. 'And were you ever involved in this ménage-à-trois?'

'Certainly not,' rebuked the doctor. 'I told you, I never met Terry.'

'Oh, so you did.' Tony knew he was being naughty, but really enjoyed making this obnoxious man squirm. 'What about Aaron?' he persisted. 'Were you ever on intimate terms with him?'

Bradbury's eyes narrowed as he answered the question crisply. 'He was a student. Only a student.'

'Well, thank you, Dr Bradbury,' responded Tony. 'You've been most helpful.'

***

At Peacock's estate and letting agency, Felicity looked at Mavis, a well-presented woman wearing a floral print blouse, a pencil skirt and bright red stiletto shoes. Mavis, the manageress of Peacock's, was very excited at the thought of being involved in a murder case. She hoped she would be called to court as a witness. 'I very much doubt that,' explained Felicity. 'All we want to know is who was the occupier of Flat 26?'

'It's not free at the moment. The police are in there. It's a crime scene.'

'I know that.' Felicity was trying hard to be patient. 'But who was in there. Who was paying the rent?'

'No one,' replied Mavis. 'It's been empty for months. Who did you say you were?'

'I didn't,' replied Felicity. She hated lying but thought it better if Mavis didn't know she was from MI5. 'I'm from E.ON. We have an outstanding account for that address.'

Mavis was visibly disappointed. She had hoped that Felicity was from the police, or maybe the press. She went over to the filing cabinet and then informed Felicity in a rather sulky voice that it was Irene Wilson.

'Have you a forwarding address?' Felicity smiled.

'Canada,' snapped Mavis.

'Canada, are you sure?' asked Felicity.

'Of course I'm sure,' Mavis replied in a somewhat indignant voice. 'From what I remember, she was planning to join her husband in Canada.'

She slammed the filing drawer closed.

***

Tony was at the sauna. He was naked, apart from a large towel around his waist. Some men were wandering around wrapped in towels, but most were nude. *I must remain professional*, thought Tony, *mustn't be tempted.* He thought about what Robert would say if he knew. He spotted someone in a tracksuit who appeared to have some authority.

'Excuse me' – Tony smiled – 'but do you know a lad here called Terry?'

'There is only one,' said the tracksuit. 'Terry O'Neal. He's over there in the steam room.'

'Thanks,' replied Tony.

'He's a good lad,' continued the tracksuit. 'Versatile.' He winked as he said this.

'Great,' said Tony. 'Just how I like 'em.' He felt guilty, but the important thing was that he fitted in and did not arouse any suspicions.

He entered the steam room. Terry O'Neal was, as far as Tony could see through the steam, a slim, dark-haired boy of about twenty. He was sitting in the steam room speaking on his mobile.

'It won't do it any good,' remarked Tony.

'What?' said the boy.

'A mobile in a steam room. It won't do it any good.'

'You're right there.' He switched the phone off.

'Are you Terry?'

'Who's asking?' was Terry's immediate response.

'A mutual friend mentioned you. Said we'd get on. All three of us would get on, if you get my meaning.'

'It's hard not to get your meaning,' replied Terry. 'So who's the mutual friend?'

'Aaron Bakha.'

Terry's demeanour suddenly changed. His streetwise cockiness was replaced by a defensive attitude. 'Aaron's dead. He was murdered.'

'Oh, I'm sorry. I didn't mean to…'

Terry stopped him. 'Poor bastard,' he said. 'Read it in the papers, didn't I? I couldn't believe it.'

'You were close friends?' said Tony tentatively, knowing he was skating on thin ice.

Terry didn't seem to notice. 'He was a good laugh, know what I mean?'

'You were together?'

'Sexually, you mean?' Terry smiled. 'No, nothing like that.'

'Was there anyone he was especially friendly with?' It was at this point that the ice broke.

'Are you from the papers?' There was a challenge in Terry's voice.

'No,' continued Tony. 'You see, Aaron was my first.' He thought that if Terry believed that, he would believe anything.

'You Arabs stick together, don't you?' Terry laughed.

If you say so, thought Tony, relieved that he seemed to have won back Terry's trust. 'So was there anyone?'

'Who he fancied; you mean? You Arabs are all the same. He liked a guy called Hassan. Don't know why, but he liked him.'

'You didn't like him?'

'No, he was too demanding, and he was creepy.'

Tony wanted to push the conversation on. 'If Aaron liked him, so may I. Do you know where Hassan lived?'

'I dunno,' responded Terry. He was beginning to lose interest.

'Anyone who would know where he lived?'

'Adam Cookson's been with him.'

'Adam?'

'He's not here at the moment. You ask a lot of questions, don't you?'

'And you open your sexy mouth and answer them,' responded Tony, knowing exactly how to play the game when necessary.

'Yes,' replied Terry. 'I guess I am pretty gobby. That's 'cos I'm upset.'

'I can see you are,' came Tony's comforting response.

'I like dirty talk,' smiled Terry, as he opened Tony's towel and went down on his knees.

Tony looked up. 'Oh, Robert, I'm sorry.'

Chapter 9

Things Become Personal

The eyes watched Charlie as she got off the bus. The eyes saw Karmel waiting for her, saw her run up to him and throw her arms around him and how he kissed her lightly on the head. They watched the pair as they walked down Shaftesbury Avenue holding hands like two young lovers.

The eyes followed them like a wild animal stalking through high grass. Eventually, Charlie and Karmel reached an Italian restaurant, walked in and were shown to a window table, where they ordered wine and food. The eyes watched them from outside as they sat talking closely, holding hands across the table. When the meal was over, they left and went back on to the avenue, where they hailed a taxi. They got in one and drove away. The eyes blinked and were gone.

***

Felicity was addressing a full incident room. She explained that she been to Peacock's Estate and Letting Agency, and they had confirmed that they handled all the flats in the property she was interested in. They had also confirmed that flat 26 had been vacant since the tenant left to join her husband in Canada. The couple had continued to pay the rent as they intended to return to the UK.

'They must be well off,' muttered Simon.

Felicity explained that the secretary had taken some time finding the spare key, blaming her colleague for putting it in the wrong drawer.

Mention of the key brought Simon into the discussion. 'Charlie's key,' he told the group, 'was on the workbench at the Hammersmith College next to the Plasticine and modelling clay. An impression of it could easily have been made.'

The group agreed that this was the most likely scenario and were interested in the fact that Peter Grainger had confirmed that some time ago the college had had a technician of North African origin working for them. At this moment, the telephone rang. Felicity answered. 'It's for you,' she announced, looking directly at Tony. 'It's Robert.'

'Robert!' exclaimed Tony. 'What the hell does he want? He never calls me at work.' He picked up the receiver.

'Sorry to trouble you at work,' said Robert. 'But I thought I'd let you know it's arrived.'

'What the hell are you talking about?' replied Tony angrily. 'What's arrived?'

'Michelangelo's statue of David. The statue you ordered from that garden centre we went to,' came Robert's innocent reply.

'I never ordered it. Just said it would look nice on the balcony.'

'Well, it's here,' responded Robert.

'What do you mean, it's here?' asked Tony.

'A big wooden box in the middle of the flat. No idea how it got in.'

The colour drained from Tony's face. He felt cold. 'Robert,' he said. 'Get out of the flat now.'

'What do you mean?' asked Robert.

'Do it,' ordered Tony. But it was too late. The phone was dead. Tony turned to the assembled group. 'He's at my flat,' he cried. 'The bastard is at my flat.'

***

Before anyone could stop him, Tony, followed by Simon, was racing down the stairs to his car. They got in and raced the short distance through the London traffic to Tony's flat. But they arrived too late. Robert was not there. The box had gone and the flat was in its usual pristine state.

Tony collapsed into a chair with his head in his hands. 'It's my fault,' he cried. 'It's all my fault.'

'Of course it's not your fault,' comforted Simon.

Tony was inconsolable. 'Robert's sensitive,' he explained in an increasingly emotional voice. 'He's not the sort of man to show aggression. He's not brave. He hates violence.'

'That doesn't mean it's your fault.'

Tony would not listen. 'I should have been more aware. I should have thought ahead.'

'How could you? You didn't know what this maniac was planning.'

'I should have done. I should have done,' continued Tony.

Simon became assertive with his boss. 'Tony, there's no point in blaming yourself.'

'What do you suggest I do?' cried Tony plaintively.

'There has to be some way of tracing him. Some clue to his whereabouts.'

Tony sat bolt upright. The emotion left him as soon as it had come. 'The Blue Lagoon,' cried Tony.

'The Blue Lagoon?' asked Simon.

'A gay sauna,' replied Tony.

'You think…?' responded Simon hesitantly.

'I'm not sure what I think, but I need an address and quickly.'

Tony stood up and left the flat. He went to his car and, accompanied by Simon, set off for the Blue Lagoon. It was a short journey from MI5 to Sloane Square, but it gave Simon the chance to express his misgivings.

'Tony,' he began. 'Do you think you're the right man to be leading this investigation now? You're too closely involved.'

Tony would have nothing of it. 'I know Robert,' he said in a determined voice. 'I'm gay. I speak Arabic. I'm the perfect man for the job. That's why Mark put me in charge in the first place.'

Simon couldn't argue with that but had a feeling of disquiet about the situation.

***

Arriving at the sauna, they were greeted by the attendant who operated the baths. He was, to say least, uncooperative, and his abrasive personality did little to warm Tony to him.

'And where do you think you're going?' he said in a loud assertive voice as the two officers entered the building. Tony flashed his identity card. 'MI5,' he said.

'I don't care if you're Boris Johnson,' said the attendant. 'You're not going in there fully clothed.'

'You don't understand,' cried Tony. The situation was really getting to him.

'No, it's you that don't understand,' persisted the attendant. 'Now put these towels on, there's good fellows, and I'll let you in for free.'

Simon had already taken the towels, and, in an attempt to defuse the situation, pushed one towards Tony. 'Put one on, mate, and let's get in there and get the information we need.'

Tony snatched the towel and they proceeded into the changing room where they were allocated a locker and a key. As they walked towards the baths, they looked into various rooms where activities were taking place that may have stimulated Tony at other times, but not on this night. He was on a mission, and nothing was going to deter him. Eventually they came to a room where Terry was sitting, gossiping to a pretty, rather petite young man. Terry looked up. 'My,' he said. 'You've returned quickly.'

Simon looked at Tony, giving him a curious stare.

'You've brought a friend,' continued Terry, looking Simon up and down. 'Very nice too.'

'I need to speak to Adam,' pleaded Tony.

'That's me,' came a soft voice from the corner. 'Terry said you wanted to speak to me.'

'You see,' smiled Terry. 'I always deliver.' He moved closer to Simon.

Tony ignored Terry, and with a directness that could only be described as abrupt, asked Adam if he knew a man called Hassan.

'That weirdo,' was Adam's response.

'You know his house?' Tony ploughed on, aiming to find out where Robert was.

'Too right I've been to his house. Didn't stay long though,' replied Adam. 'I felt uncomfortable, so when he went to the toilet, I took my leave.'

'Why? What was so wrong with him?' interrupted Simon, who was feeling the pressure of Terry's fingers running down his back.

'He was on about what we did being wrong,' said Adam. 'I said it may be wrong for you, mate, but I love it, and it pays the rent.'

He started getting really agitated. 'Wrong for Muslims,' he said. 'Wrong for Muslims to do what we're doing.' I tell you, man, he was getting really heated.'

'Do you know where he lives?' persisted Tony.

'Ealing. St Leonard's Road.'

'What number?' asked Tony.

'No idea.'

'Would you know it if I took you there?'

'Guess so,' replied Adam.

'Here's fifty quid. Put your clothes on.'

'I normally get that for taking them off.'

'Yes, well, consider it a treat.'

Tony moved out of the room with Adam following.

'Can I come too?' cried Terry.

'If you must,' responded Tony.

Simon wished that Tony had said no, which in normal times he would have done, but all his thoughts were for Robert.

***

72

In the car, Adam sat in the passenger seat, and Terry sat in the back with Simon. No sooner had they got in than Simon could feel the pressure of Terry's hand on his knee. He would have stopped him if the situation had been usual, but it was not, and he realised he had to keep the two boys on board. He decided that he would quickly restrict Terry's activities if they progressed beyond being friendly. To him, the journey to Ealing seemed to take hours, although it was only about half an hour.

'This is St Leonard's Road,' cried Adam. It was a road of large Victorian houses which, in their day, must have been quite aristocratic, but now showed the sad neglect of multiple occupancies.

'I'm not too sure which is the house,' whined Adam.

'You said you'd know,' snarled Tony.

'I did, but now I've forgotten. Wait a minute. Go back a bit,' instructed Adam. 'There, that house with the Pakistani flag in the window.'

Tony ordered the much-relieved Simon out of the car and gave the two boys £20 and told them to get a taxi back to the baths.

'You've already given them fifty,' protested Simon.

Tony wasn't listening. He was more interested in finding the flat.

The main door of the house was locked. Tony rang the first flat doorbell, and, after a while, it was opened by a woman in her thirties who was expecting a takeaway delivery. Tony ignored her protestations, showed his warrant card and charged up the stairs, leaving Simon to apologise for his curtness.

There were three doors on the first-floor landing, and, working out which had the Pakistani flag, Tony went to it. To his surprise, the door was not locked. He carefully entered the flat. It was typical of a London bedsit: woodchip on the walls, junk furniture bought at an auction, nothing personal. The flat was empty, apart from a large crate in the centre of one of the rooms. Tony trembled as he approached it. He knew what could be inside, and didn't want to find out. It was then that Simon took over. 'Here, let me open it, sir.'

Tony didn't resist; he knew it was for the best. Simon opened the crate, and a decapitated body fell out. To Tony's relief, it was not Robert. The man was Arabic; Tony had no doubt it was Hassan. He fell on his knees and cried, 'It's not him, it's not him,' repeating it over and over again.

'If that's not Robert, then where the hell is he?' asked Simon. 'Could he have escaped?'

'No, he's not the adventurous type,' responded Tony. 'He'd be terrified, and he certainly wouldn't decapitate a man and put his body in a crate. No, if he's gone, he's been taken. The question is, by whom.'

'I'll ring Bullock and keep him in the loop,' said Simon. 'The Met can take over this part of the inquiry, though they'll still want to know about Robert.'

'Call them,' responded Tony, 'and then let's get back to the office.'

***

They arrived back at the office, Tony feeling relieved. Robert had been taken, but at least he wasn't in the hands of some psychotic psychopath.

'It is quite common practice in the Middle East for a hostage to be sold on from one group to another,' explained Tony. 'Only in this case he wasn't sold; he was taken. They, whoever they are, have taken him as a bargaining tool. For what, we do not know yet. One thing we do know is, he's more useful to them alive than dead. Otherwise, we would have found his body.'

'But why kill Hassan?' asked Simon.

'He was a loose cannon. Obviously disliked by the Muslim brothers for trying to hijack the Muslim cause.'

Their discussion was suddenly interrupted by Felicity. 'Sir,' she cried. 'There's something coming through from Lebanon and Al Jazeera.'

On the screen there was the image of a soldier on his knees. Behind him was a man in black with a large knife and a machete, and behind him was the ISIS flag.

The man in black said, 'I speak to you from London, England, the so-called land of the free. The country that has been at war with the Muslim world for the last one thousand years. A country that oppressed our people for centuries and is now waking up to a new dawn.'

He then ordered the soldier to speak. The strange thing about the soldier was that he was dark, probably a Muslim. He spoke, obviously under duress. 'My name is Private Michael Jones of the Royal Engineers. Britain is doomcd. Soldiers, forget your allegiance to Queen and country. You may be free today, but you will be slaves tomorrow.'

What happened next was incredible. The man in black lifted his machete. Felicity closed her eyes, expecting the worst. But nothing happened. Silence. The man in black turned to the camera. 'I could do it if I wished, but I do not wish. That is the power of Islam. Those who go against our brotherhood will be punished; others will be shown mercy.'

The group sat bemused. Felicity was the first to speak. 'Do you think this broadcast has a connection with the…?' She stopped herself from saying 'beheading'. 'Well, what we found this morning?'

'Undoubtedly,' explained Tony, 'the execution of Hassan was for his betrayal of Islam by not only acting on his own but being both a sinner and a hypocrite. According to Muslim teaching, the man who condemns a man for a sin which he himself has committed is the greater sinner. While the soldier, though in the British army, has been shown compassion. I think he will, however, have to renounce his allegiance to the crown.'

'So you think there is a link between the abduction of Robert and this rather nasty broadcast?'

'I do,' replied Tony. 'There is a link and we have to find it. Who was indirectly connected to the previous murders? Do any names spring out at us?'

'Charlie Briggs. She knew Hassan, and leased the workshop where Richardson was found,' replied Mike Bailey.

'Tenuous, but true,' mused Tony.

'Not so tenuous,' declared Simon. 'I've been looking at her behaviour, and there's definitely something wrong.'

'Meaning?' questioned Tony.

'Well, when she found the body of Richardson, she was shocked and upset. Her grief was not put on. But her attitude to authority, and Bullock in particular, was challenging and defensive.'

'A lot of people aren't happy with authority,' put in Tony. 'The police in particular, and Bullock most definitely.'

'That's true,' agreed Simon. 'But take a look at the photos and the inventory from the crime scene.'

Everyone looked, not sure of what they were supposed to find.

'You see,' explained Simon, 'an industrial sewing machine; a large table for cutting out patterns and materials; and a sofa bed, which Charlie says she uses when she has a big order on and can't be bothered to cycle home.'

'Fair enough,' shrugged Tony.

'Hear me out,' insisted Simon. 'There's a sink, an electric kettle and a stack of old paintings. But there are no textiles. No rolls of material, no reams of cloth. She's a textile designer. Where are the fabrics she works with? Sure, she may have just finished an order, but there would still be some rolls left over, and usually, in such workshops, there's a dustbin full of remnants. But here, nothing.'

'Yes,' Tony agreed. 'Strange.'

'What is more,' went on Simon, 'she's living far beyond her means. Her rent is 1500 pounds a month for her flat, and she pays 800 pounds a month for the lock-up. Where does it all come from? Roger's looked into her account. Her rent goes out on the 25th of the month, and the money to cover it goes in on the 24th.'

'Well, let's check who's paying in the money,' replied Tony.

'We can't,' said Simon in a resigned manner. 'She pays cash in on the 24th; there is no way we can trace it. There is no paper trail.'

Tony put the photo of the crime scene down and gave out orders. 'Flick, find out all you can about Charlie Briggs and Peter Grainger, and make a list of all tenants in the flat where the murders took place to see if anyone had a link with Hassan.' He turned to Simon. 'Thanks, Simon. The Met's loss is our gain. That was a brilliant piece of detection. I want you to find Charlie Briggs and give her an in-depth interview.'

'She said her mother was coming to take her home,' replied Simon. 'I'll find her mother's address and visit her there.'

'You do that,' agreed Tony. 'I'm going to the Haroun Al Rashid.'

'Oh, the Muslim wine bar.' Keith spoke out in his usual thoughtless manner.

'You're wrong,' corrected Tony. 'They are Muslims, so no alcohol. It'll be what it says, a coffee bar. I'll go there and see what their reaction is to the beheading.'

Chapter 10
Someone's Not Telling the Truth

Simon thought the Briggs' living room was a throwback to the 1970s. A musky-pink Dralon three-piece suite dominated the room. This was complemented by a pink and green floral Axminster carpet, rose velvet curtains, and some Lladro ornaments in a mahogany cabinet. Everything had its place. Simon was quite sure that the room was dusted and vacuumed every day. Mrs Briggs was in the kitchen making a pot of tea. Her husband, a tall, thin gentleman, well-dressed in a shirt, slacks, and the requisite carpet slippers, sat opposite Simon and spoke with great passion on his favourite sport, cricket. He told Simon, without being rude, that he hoped the meeting wouldn't last too long as he was waiting for the cricket transmission from Australia.

'Wonderful, this technology,' smiled Simon.

Mr Briggs agreed. 'Indeed it is.'

Mrs Briggs entered with a tray on which was a pretty Royal Doulton tea service, obviously kept for best, a plate of shortbread biscuits, and three side plates. Mrs Briggs was a small, neat-looking woman, wearing a floral smock and fluffy blue slippers. It was obvious that she took great pride in her appearance as she had well-manicured nails, and Simon suspected that she visited the hairdresser's once a week.

'How do you like your tea?' asked Mrs Briggs.

'Milk, no sugar,' replied Simon.

She offered her husband a biscuit and warned him not to drop any crumbs on the floor. Simon refused a biscuit, fearing that he may indeed drop crumbs on the spotless floor.

After busying herself with the pouring and distribution of the tea, Mrs Briggs sat carefully on a chair opposite Simon. 'It's lovely having visitors,' she said. 'Isn't it, Brian? We don't get many.' She paused for a moment, and then informed Simon that her name was Maureen. Another pause, and then, after taking a sip of tea, she asked him why they had the honour of a visit from MI5. She had wanted to say, a visit from such a handsome young man, but thought that would be a bit forward.

'Well, it's not you that I came to see,' started Simon, 'but your daughter.'

Mrs Briggs looked shocked, and her husband put down the newspaper he had started to read.

'I'm afraid Charlotte isn't here at the moment,' responded Mrs Briggs. 'Indeed, it's several months since we've seen her. I hope she's not in any trouble.'

'No trouble, Mrs Briggs. But Charlie, I mean Charlotte,' Simon corrected himself, not wanting to get into trouble with the fastidious Mrs Briggs, 'said that you were picking her up in the car after the incident.'

'No,' replied Maureen. 'I haven't picked her up. I don't drive. Brian, my husband, is the only one who drives. We've just got a new Honda Civic. Brian's very pleased with it, aren't you, love?' She suddenly stopped, realising what Simon had said. 'Incident?' she cried. 'What incident?'

Simon felt he had wasted enough time, and his response was rather blunt. 'A man was found murdered in your daughter's workshop.' He did not think it necessary to say how the man had been murdered. The very word murder was enough to disturb Mrs Briggs.

Simon thought the house-proud lady from West Ruislip was going to drop the cup of tea on her well-swept carpet. 'How dreadful,' she said. Did Charlotte know the man?'

'We don't think so,' reassured Simon.

'And did Charlotte find the murdered man?'

'We believe he was a stranger.'

'How terrible,' continued Mrs Briggs. Then, with a puzzled look, she asked a very pertinent question. 'Fancy telling you that I'd pick her up when she knew I didn't drive. Why would she say that?'

'Why indeed?' replied Simon.

Mr Briggs spoke for the first time. 'Because she was contrary. Stubborn. Like her mother. She most likely had a secret that she didn't want you to know.'

'What secret?' Simon picked up on this.

'How the hell should I know? We haven't seen her for at least a year.'

'I thought your wife said it was several months.'

'Contrary. See what I mean? You can't believe either of them.'

'I see,' said Simon, realising that the tension was mounting in the room. 'It does raise a question. If you, Mr Briggs, didn't pick her up, then who did?'

'Wouldn't know,' said Briggs gruffly. 'She didn't keep in touch. She changed when she went to that university.'

'She got very picky over what she'd eat,' interjected Mrs Briggs. 'There were weeks when she refused to eat anything at all.'

'Your daughter went to university to study textiles?' asked Simon.

'She went to Chelsea College to study textiles. She was always very artistic,' clarified Charlie's mother. 'It was while she was there that she became interested in politics.' She chuckled. 'Wanted to be a member of parliament, she did.'

'Really, for what party?' asked Simon.

'The Liberal Democrats. Daddy used to mock her, didn't you, Brian? He used to say, "If you want to stand for parliament, at least stand for a party that has a chance of getting in." But she didn't listen. She loved Shirley Williams. I think it was her voice she liked. She used to say that when she got older, she would like to be as articulate as Shirley Williams. She really admired her.'

'Then what happened?' asked Simon.

'Brian's mother died,' explained Maureen. 'Daddy was very fond of his mother, weren't you?' Brian picked up his newspaper, not wanting to be associated with his wife's embarrassing babble. 'Anyway,' continued Maureen. 'The long and the short of it was that his mother left Charlotte some money. You see, Charlotte was her only grandchild.'

'Was it a large amount of money?' asked Simon, not wishing to sound indiscreet.

'Enough to put her through university.'

'Did that please you?'

'Not really,' replied Maureen. 'She'd already got her degree in textiles. Why did she want another degree? She was artistic, clever with her hands. With the money her gran had left she could have opened her own business.'

'Which one?' queried Simon.

Mrs Briggs looked confused. 'Which one? What do you mean?'

Mr Briggs put his paper down impatiently. 'The man's asking you which university Charlotte went to.'

'Oh, yes, of course,' replied Maureen, feeling duly reprimanded by her husband. 'She went to Nottingham University to study politics and sociology.'

'It was while she was at university that she changed,' grumbled Brian.

'Changed in what way?' enquired Simon.

'She was happy enough in the first year,' said Maureen, sounding nostalgic. 'In her second year, she became quiet and distant. No longer interested in the Lib Dems, not even interested in Shirley Williams. When she left university, we thought she'd come back to Ruislip. But no,' there was sadness in Maureen's voice. 'She wanted her independence, and we hardly ever saw her after that.'

'I'm sorry,' said Simon with real pity in his voice. 'Can you tell me, did she join any groups while at uni?'

Maureen shook her head. 'I don't know. As I told you, she didn't talk.'

'What about friends?' persisted Simon.

Brian put his paper down. He was obviously getting impatient. 'My wife told you she became secretive, didn't talk. Yes, she may have had friends, but she never mentioned them to us.'

'I'm sorry we can't be more helpful,' apologised Maureen.

'On the contrary, you've been very helpful,' smiled Simon. 'I will now leave you in peace to watch the cricket,' and with that, he left.

As Simon drove away, the plaintive face of a young woman looked out of the dormer window.

***

Tony sat at a table in the Haroun Al Rashid bar, drinking coffee and holding a paper as though reading it. To say he was actually reading it would be inaccurate. There was no way he could think of anything but Robert, and where he might be. It was not long, however, before he was approached. 'Ah, my friend, good to see you.'

Tony looked up, recognised him as the man from his previous encounter, and replied that he was pleased to see him.

'You're in a suit,' said the man.

'I'm at work. One has to earn a living,' replied Tony.

The man showed some interest, asking Tony where he worked. Tony told him that he worked at an insurance company and that it was very boring. They sat for a moment and Tony decided that he was not prepared for another afternoon of small talk. He wanted answers and he was not prepared to mess around.

'We chat,' said Tony. 'But I know nothing about you.'

'Why should you?' replied the man.

'No reason,' declared Tony. 'But it would be good to know your name.'

'Haroun. And yours?'

'Tony Assad. My Moroccan name is Ali.'

'Ali Assad,' smiled Haroun. 'And I bet you speak Arabic.'

'Of course,' smiled Tony. 'You are called Haroun?'

The man cut in. 'Haroun Al Rashid.'

'The same name as the bar,' said Tony, attempting a look of surprise.

'I am the bar,' announced Haroun proudly.

Tony continued to look incredulous. 'You own the bar? You're a man of many secrets, Haroun Al Rashid.'

'Indeed,' responded Haroun. 'The question is, are you?'

'Am I what?' asked Tony innocently.

'A man of many secrets,' came the reply.

'One or two.' There was a silence. 'The brothers are not here today?'

'It is not Friday.'

'I thought that maybe after the execution…'

Haroun smiled. 'I am not sure.' There was a pause. Tony took a sip of his coffee, his eyes always on Haroun. Haroun continued. 'Ali Assad, good Islamic name, speaks fluent Arabic.'

Tony corrected him. 'I never said it was fluent.'

'You are always asking questions,' Haroun continued, ignoring Tony's interruption. 'Should I trust you, brother?'

Tony looked Haroun in the eye. 'Should I trust you, brother?' There was a silence, and then both men burst out laughing. But even in their mirth, they felt little trust in each other.

***

On leaving Haroun, Tony decided to visit the flat in St Leonard's Road, Ealing, where Hassan had been so brutally killed. A cursory look showed nothing. Then, exploring one of the drawers containing clothes, he found, underneath the lining paper, a small photograph of three students, one female and two males. One of the male students had his arm around the girl. Tony muttered to himself about how thorough the Met were, and proceeded to call Felicity.

'Ah, Flick,' he said. 'Tony. Will you do me a search on a David Green. He may be known as Kamel Ghaffar or Haroun Al Rashid. Came from Leeds, I believe. I want you to see if you can find a photo of him.'

'Will do,' replied Felicity cheerily. 'By the way, I have some interesting information regarding Charlie Briggs.'

'Keep it until I get back,' snapped Tony. 'I'll be in the office in thirty minutes.'

***

At the same time, Simon, on leaving the Briggs' family home, decided to pay a visit to Peter Grainger at his flat in Ravenscourt Park.

Peter was about thirty-five, quite ordinary looking considering he was an art teacher. No long hair, no piercings, in fact, nothing hippie about him at all. His flat, though modest, was well cared for and reasonably tidy. He apologised for being unable to be more helpful about Charlie. 'She was a vegetarian, never used bad language and kept herself to herself.'

'So she wasn't unfriendly, standoffish?' asked Simon.

'No, not at all. She was very helpful and very skilful. A good laugh, really.'

'Any friends?' insisted Simon.

'Not that I am aware of.'

'How about you?'

'Me? Charlie's boyfriend? Good heavens, no.'

'When I first met you at the college,' continued Simon, 'you mentioned a technician you thought was of North African descent. Was Charlie friendly with him?'

'I really wouldn't know. They used to talk. I believe they were at university together.'

Simon smiled. 'Thanks Peter, you've been very helpful.'

***

Back in the incident room, Tony prepared to brief the troops.

'So,' he began, 'we've found a link between Hassan and Charlie Briggs. They both met at a Muslim group while they were at Nottingham University.'

'And it was there that they were radicalised?' added Simon.

'Maybe,' agreed Tony. 'While searching Hassan's room, in a drawer I found a photo of a group of students taken at university.' Tony asked Flick if she had found a photo of David Green. She produced his university identity photograph, which she projected onto a large screen. 'David is rather reluctant to have his photo taken. This is the only one I could find,' she added.

'Could you put a beard on him?' asked Tony.

'What type of beard? A Van Dyke or a Brian Blessed?' asked Felicity.

'Let's try the Brian Blessed,' smiled Tony. 'As I thought, my friend from the Haroun Al Rashid.'

'It means,' said Simon, 'that if you know who he is, he will undoubtedly know who you are.'

'I must go to the bar,' declared Tony, but was stopped by Felicity.

'Go,' she said, 'but not before you've heard what I have to tell you.' She took centre stage. 'You asked me to search into Charlie's past, and I discovered that she has an older sister.'

Simon looked shocked. 'Mrs Briggs never mentioned any sister.'

'Did you ask her?' questioned Tony.

'Well, no,' replied Simon. 'I thought Charlie was an only child.'

'She wouldn't mention her,' continued Felicity. 'Mrs Briggs has been married twice, and Charlie's half-sister, Alina, was to Mrs Briggs' first husband, Oleg Rebrov.'

'Obviously not English,' observed Mike.

'Obviously,' continued Felicity. 'He was from Ukraine and lectured in Russian literature at London University.'

'What happened to him?' enquired Simon.

'Nothing happened to him, he's still alive,' said Felicity, feeling slightly smug with herself for digging up so much information. 'He divorced Maureen in 1995 and married again in 2000. He has two children to his wife Stephanie, and lives in a large detached house in Richmond overlooking the park.'

'Does he still work for the university?' asked Mike.

'No. He retired from the world of academia two years ago at the age of sixty-five.'

Tony had been silent during this revelation, but now he spoke.

'You say he came from Ukraine. Whereabouts?'

Felicity wasn't expecting this question and had to look at her notes. 'The Crimean Peninsula,' she answered eventually.

'Of course,' replied Tony. 'It would have to be.' It was at this point that Tony realised the truth.

Chapter 11

Tony had watched those TV crime dramas where the leading investigator gets too involved with the personality of the criminal and starts acting irrationally. Screaming, kicking doors, and behaving in what he considered an absurd manner that would never be tolerated or allowed to happen in reality. He was determined that he was not going to behave in that way, despite his closeness to the victim. He did, however, feel a real dread of going back to his flat, the flat he had shared with Robert for the past five years. An empty flat, with no conversation, no arguments, and, worst of all, an empty bedroom. How could he lie in their bed, warm and comfortable but alone, not knowing where Robert may be, and if he was suffering? He knew Robert would be terrified. The office was emptying, and the moment was approaching when he would have to leave. Oh God, do I have to go home? Shall I go to a bar and get very drunk? It was at this point that Simon approached him. Simon appeared to have read his mind.

Simon knew he mustn't mention Robert, or Tony's feeling of loss, so he took another tack. 'Hey mate, you look lost in a world of your own.'

'Yes,' replied Tony, in a dull voice. 'Just thinking about the case.'

'Wondered if you'd like to come around to ours for the evening. I'm sure Sarah would soon rustle up some food for us.'

'Sarah?' asked Tony, realising he'd never asked Simon the name of his wife.

'If she can't,' continued Simon, 'I could always ring for a takeaway.'

'Thanks,' replied Tony. 'We can call at a supermarket and I'll buy some wine.'

'No need,' was Simon's reply, but Tony insisted. As they were on their way out, the phone on Tony's desk rang. Tony picked up the receiver, murmuring, 'Who the hell can that be?'

'Is that Ali Assad, or should I call you Tony?' said the caller.

Tony, though taken off guard, responded quickly. 'Haroun! Or should I call you David?'

Haroun gave a dry, quick laugh. 'Look, brother, I'll cut to the chase. The brothers want to meet with you at the bar at seven tonight. Please be prompt.' The phone went silent.

Tony related the message to Simon, who was concerned that it could be a trap. But Tony would have none of it. He was fired with enthusiasm.

'A trap?' he said. 'No, if they want to meet with me, it's for a reason. What the reason is, I've no idea.'

'I'll take you. They don't know my car, and I can wait for you.'

'If you wouldn't mind,' agreed Tony.

'I wouldn't have offered if I'd minded,' smiled his obliging partner.

***

Tony walked through the door of the Haroun Al Rashid at precisely 7 pm. Three brothers sat at a table. The man in the centre, the Imam, was obviously the leader of and spokesperson for the group. He spoke quietly, but with authority. 'Please sit down, Mr Assad.'

Tony sat down and took a quick look around what appeared to be a deserted bar. 'Haroun is not here?'

The Imam replied that Haroun was busy with other work. He cleared his throat and began to speak. 'Mr Assad, let us make it clear from the start that we know exactly who you are.' He looked in a file. 'Tony Assad, MI5 agent, working on the North African desk. Recruited from Oxford University Centre for Islamic Studies, after achieving a first in that subject at London University.' He looked up and smiled. 'A highly qualified young man. You are of Moroccan descent. Your grandparents were Moroccan, and you visit Morocco on a regular basis to see relatives, and this has enabled you to read Arabic and speak it fluently.'

'You forgot to mention that my mother's English,' replied Tony.

'We know who your mother is.' He smiled, trying to show a little humour. 'I watch her cookery programme.'

Tony was quite sure that he did not but wanted to keep up the cheerful banter. 'You have researched me very well. Don't tell me you are trying to recruit my services.'

'In the future, who knows?' The Imam suddenly changed tone and became serious. 'Mr Assad, you must understand that we are here to help the Muslim community in the UK. We are here to help our brothers, and to try to point them in the right direction.' There was a pause. He took a sip of water from the glass in front of him. 'There is a group of my brothers,' he continued, 'who hold your friend Robert. This group is prepared to offer his safe return, if you are able to do something for them.'

Tony's relaxed and laid-back attitude, engendered in the earlier part of the conversation, suddenly changed to a tense one. 'What do they want?' he demanded.

'I understand there is a special envoy arriving in this country in the next couple of days from the United States, with important papers relating to the war in Syria. These papers are being taken to your prime minister and foreign secretary. It would be very helpful for us to view these papers.'

'You've got the wrong man,' said Tony. 'I'm an agent, not a politician or a civil servant. There is no way I could get near those papers.'

'Quite so, quite so, we understand that,' replied the Imam, in a soothing voice. 'All we want to know is, when the envoy arrives, and where.'

'That would be difficult,' responded Tony.

'Difficult but not impossible.' The Imam closed the file. 'Mr Assad, your friend is in a distressed state. I suggest you try to help.'

'Don't hurt him, please don't hurt him,' pleaded Tony.

The Imam looked shocked. 'Mr Assad, as well you know, and despite western propaganda to the contrary, the Islamic people are civilised, and your friend will be well looked after whilst in our care.'

Tony was relieved to hear that but wanted the answer to one question. 'Why did you feel it necessary to kill Hassan? Why not render him unconscious and hand him over to the police. Why decapitate him?'

'Your friend was being held by an unreasonable man; what I think you call a psychopath. We tried to negotiate with him, but he would have none of it. He wanted nothing more than to kill your friend. There was a struggle. Unfortunately, one of our men got over-zealous and Hassan ended up on the floor. It was an accident.' The Imam shook his head. 'He was a very sick man. After his death, our men, on their own initiative, decided to stage what had happened as an execution. I really have no idea why they should have taken such an unpleasant step.' He shook his head again. 'I lead them, Mr Assad, but I cannot dictate to them.'

After those sobering words, Tony left the bar.

***

Sarah Newlove was a small, delicate young woman with blonde flowing hair, petite features and the most delightful smile. She was thrilled that Simon had brought Tony to the house. 'I've so wanted to meet you,' she cried. 'Simon does nothing but talk about you.'

'Sarah, please,' said a somewhat embarrassed Simon.

'I hope you liked the paella, not as good as your mother makes, I'm sure. Chicken and chorizo, as well as the usual prawns and mussels.'

'It was delicious,' said Tony.

'Really? Oh dear, I think I'm talking too much. It's nerves.'

'Yes, you are talking rather a lot, darling, and at a considerable rate of knots.'

'I'm afraid I haven't a sweet, though there is some cheese in the fridge. Would you think it awfully rude of me if I left you, two men, alone? There's a programme on television at nine that I desperately want to watch.'

'Not at all,' responded Tony. 'Simon and I have things to talk about anyway.'

'Good. Simon, will you get the cheese out. There's Cheddar in the fridge, and Double Gloucester and Brie on the board at room temperature. Cheese biscuits in the cupboard.' With that, a very flustered Sarah left the room. Simon got out two side plates, knives, cheese and a bottle of good red wine. He took out a bottle of whisky for later in the evening. Tony smiled, appreciative of the effort they were making, but feeling desperately guilty about Robert and wondering where he was.

Robert was actually sitting at a table with two other men, eating couscous, a lamb tagine and flatbread. The terror of the actual kidnapping had left him. He was still nervous, but his hosts were friendly and joked with him. He realised he was a hostage, but at this moment he was not in fear for his life.

Simon and Tony settled down with a full glass of wine each and a plate of cheese. They started to discuss and dissect the day's dramas.

'Tell me,' started Simon, 'what exactly you meant by saying that it would have to be, when you learnt that Oleg Rebrov had come from the Crimean Peninsula.'

Tony took a sip of the wine, thought for a moment, and then put forward his theory. 'Ukraine has a complex political history. I'm sure you know that up to 1991, it was part of the USSR. In 1991 it became an independent state. It was, and has always been, an uncomfortable situation for it with big brother Russia always looking over its shoulder. In 2014, with the expansion of the European Union, the government of Ukraine in Kiev made an application to join the European family. This did not please Russia. It didn't please Russia at all. Areas of Ukraine, Muslim areas, were equally unhappy about this attempt to join forces with Europe. This displeasure led, in the later part of 2014, to the annexing of part of Ukraine by Russia, thus returning it to its control. The part annexed, as I am sure you have guessed,' explained Tony, 'was the Crimean Peninsula. Today, the Russian Orthodox religion is still the prominent religion of Ukraine. It is, however, estimated that 300,000 Muslims live in the annexed state and they feel divided from, and mistrustful of, those in the part that wasn't annexed. You see, Simon, they are unlike the Muslims of Europe, who came to our land looking for work and a good life. These Muslims saw themselves as the indigenous population. After all, they had lived there for several thousand years. They were Sunni Muslims, proud of their Tartar descent, and they felt betrayed by what they saw as the weak governments of the west. The autocratic rule of Russia was more the style of government they were used to. All over North Africa, democracy was in short supply, and what most countries understood and respected was dictatorship. Who knows, if Saddam Hussein and General Gaddafi had not been deposed, we may have seen a fragile peace in the Middle East. True, they had cruel laws, but they were laws and punishments that the population understood. Do you honestly believe if Saddam or Gaddafi were in power, there would have been any place for ISIS?'

The talking went on. Sarah went to bed, and the men started on the whisky.

'You're still not telling me everything, are you?' questioned Simon.

'What do you mean?'

'You're holding out on me regarding our present situation.'

Tony sighed. 'There are a group of Muslim men in Europe, indeed around the world – academics, politicians, and intellectuals – who are fighting for Islam. Not fighting in the literal sense. These men do not promote violence, but their aim is the same as that of the jihadists. They want a balanced Muslim world, a more integrated world. And sometimes, like ostriches, they bury their heads in the sand when violent acts of terrorism take place. They don't condone it, but they understand it, and they pray for the day when there won't be any need for Islamic terrorism.'

'And you believe Oleg Rebrov could be one of these men? A group that neither supports nor condemns atrocities?' questioned Simon.

'Could be. The question is, how does he fit in and how do his girls fit in? The picture is not complete,' remarked Tony.

'Tell me,' said Simon, 'how do you know so much about this organisation?'

Tony turned and looked straight into Simon's eyes. 'My father was one of the men. He worked all his life with British intelligence and with the Muslim brothers, to achieve tolerance and understanding.'

'Racism is a nasty thing.'

'No,' corrected Tony. 'The young Muslim men who kick off about slogans and verbal abuse are understandable. The racism my father deplored was the racism developed over hundreds of years in the British, French and Belgian empires, and handed down through the ages by such as her Imperial Majesty's colonies and the Commonwealth. It is handed down in such a way that we see it as normal and acceptable.'

Simon decided it was better not to discuss the matter any further. Tony was getting too sensitive. Simon had hit on a very tender nerve. He therefore asked Tony how Mark would react to the imam's request.

'How do you think?' sneered Tony. 'He will refuse.'

'So?' questioned Simon.

'I have my own ideas.' He swallowed another glassful of whisky and slumped.

'Come on, old man,' cried Simon. 'It's time you went to bed.'

'No,' insisted Tony. 'I must go home.'

'Not tonight, mate. You can go home tomorrow. Tonight you're sleeping in our spare room.'

Chapter 12

A Visit to Richmond Park

'No, absolutely not,' said Mark, berating Tony.

'But, Mark, you're not listening,' argued Tony, becoming exasperated with Dame Edna's lack of understanding.

'Oh, I do understand. You want me to compromise this department by disclosing state secrets.'

'No, I'm not asking you to do anything of the sort,' explained Tony, who was trying to remain calm. 'What I'm asking for is a decoy. A false delegation made up of special forces. But we would have to know the date, time and location of the real one so there could be no conflict.'

'Our men could get killed,' replied Mark, sticking to his guns.

'Yes, they could,' agreed Tony. 'But the chances would be in our favour. We would have the advantage of surprise and foreknowledge.'

Mark was not giving up. 'When they find out, they'll kill your boyfriend.'

Tony became angry. 'Will you please stop calling him my boyfriend as though it's something dirty.'

'The fact remains that he'll be killed.'

Tony spoke calmly. 'Don't you think I haven't thought of that? If I don't deliver what they ask for, he will certainly be killed. This way, well, at least I have a couple of extra days to find him.'

Mark mused for a while, and then looked up, and told Tony that he would ring the old woman.

Tony left the office, pleased that he'd achieved a little victory, only to be greeted by Felicity. 'I've just had a really odd call from Peacock's estate agents. I asked the lady in charge to keep me informed if there were any odd lettings or leasing, and she just got back to me with a message to say that Charlie Briggs has extended the lease on her workshop.'

'What's odd about that?' interrupted Simon.

Felicity's reply was simple. 'I wouldn't have thought she'd want to keep it after what happened.'

'True,' considered Tony. 'But it could be used as a holding place or a film location. Just think of it. To use a crime scene as a secure venue is a brilliant idea.'

'Since the death of Hassan, it is no longer a crime scene,' commented Simon.

Tony's first impulse was to go charging to the lock-up straight away. But he held back, fearing it would not only put Robert's life in danger, but also ruin the whole operation. Instead, he told the group that he wanted 24-hour surveillance on the workshop. 'Robert may be held there, or he may not, but I'm not going to take any chances.'

After giving instructions to his team on the jobs he wished doing, he left with Simon to visit Oleg Rebrov in his luxurious house overlooking Richmond Park.

***

Oleg could not have been more welcoming, as he invited Tony and Simon into his house. He was tall, smartly dressed, and 67 years old. Tony thought he was jovial for a Russian. They were ushered from a large hall into a beautifully decorated drawing room. The ornate gilt furniture and red silk walls were decadent enough, but what stood out dramatically was a large painting over the fireplace. It was the face of John Lennon. The face contained religious iconic art showing monks praying in cloisters, angels' wings, and a boy playing a guitar. Simon and Tony found their eyes drawn to it. 'That's an amazing piece of art,' complimented Simon.

'Yes, painted by my fellow countryman, Oleg Shupliak. Same name Oleg, same country Ukraine, but unfortunately not the same politics.'

Tony was about to make a comment on Oleg's statement but considered it better to let it rest. He wanted to ease himself into Oleg's trust and did not want to let him veer off on some vague political tangent.

'Tea?' Oleg asked, as he pressed a button on the wall.

'Thanks,' said Tony. He wondered if he had ever seen one of these Victorian-era buttons used in real life. He thought they were mostly disabled and defunct. As they sat down, a young lady entered the room. 'Can you make tea for three, Olga?' asked Oleg graciously. The girl smiled and left the room. 'I am sure it amuses you that a man from the former USSR should live in such decadence. It amuses me also, but I do it because I feel entitled to do so.'

'I envy you,' commented Simon.

'I am so pleased you have come. I was going to inform the police, but when I was told that someone from MI5 was to visit me, I thought I'd hold off making the call.'

'You were going to call the police? May I ask why, Mr Rebrov?' asked Tony.

'My daughter Alina has gone missing,' replied Oleg.

'How old is your daughter?' asked Tony.

'Twenty-seven years old. Why does that matter?' Oleg cried sharply.

'Simply because a lady of that age is her own woman. We have no powers to investigate her failure to return home.'

'She has been gone for four nights. It is most unlike her.'

'Maybe she's staying with friends,' commented Simon.

'She has no friends,' stated Oleg abruptly.

At this point, Olga entered the room with a pot of tea, cups, saucers, milk and sugar. 'Sliced lemon, but no shortbread.'

'Thank you, Olga,' said Oleg politely. The girl left the room. 'You must understand that Alina is not a girl like most girls, you know. For a start, she is super intelligent, but with the intelligence comes naivety.'

'Do you think she may have a boyfriend?'

'About four weeks ago,' continued Oleg, 'she brought home a young man called Hassan. Hassan Moffitt. A nice boy, quiet, polite, very courteous. I liked him. I was overjoyed to think my Alina had at last met a boy she was fond of. Now I read that he has committed terrible crimes and my daughter is missing.'

'Mr Rebrov,' responded Tony comfortingly. 'If it is that Hassan, and it very well could be, I doubt he would have committed any crime against your daughter.'

'I know what you are saying. I am aware of the situation. But what if his shame led to resentment towards my daughter.'

'Does your other daughter know?'

'If you are referring to Alina's half-sister, then I must tell you that she is not my daughter. We rarely speak.' It was a curt reply, which shocked both men.

'What about your ex-wife? Would she know the whereabouts of Alina?' asked Tony.

'I very much doubt it. I haven't seen Maureen for several years. The divorce was not harmonious.'

'Could I ask,' went on Tony, realising he was about to walk on eggshells, 'where you first met Maureen?'

Oleg looked up, surprised at the question. 'She was one of my students.'

Simon was shocked. 'You mean Maureen studied Russian literature?'

If Oleg was affronted, he did not show it. 'Yes, why not?' he responded. 'She speaks excellent Russian.'

Simon was very shocked. That prim little lady who gave him tea in Royal Doulton cups and worried about crumbs being dropped on the floor was an academic who spoke fluent Russian. The two images did not connect. But then the portrait of John Lennon did not seem to have a connection with a Muslim academic who lectured in Russian literature.

'Mr Rebrov, we shall, of course, report to you if we find Alina. That is, of course, if she agrees that we inform you. As she is an adult, we have to observe her right to privacy. That was not, however, why we are here today,' continued Tony.

'No?' responded Oleg, looking puzzled.

'No, it's about your other daughter, Charlotte.'

'As I said, she is not my daughter. Our relationship is not good.'

'And why is that?' asked Tony.

'Charlotte was born in 1997.' Oleg made the statement as though it should mean something to the two men. It did not. He continued, 'It was in 1996 that Maureen and I separated. Charlotte was born in May. Not to put too fine a point on it, Charlotte is not my child.'

'Oh, I understand. At least I think I do,' said Tony, trying to puzzle the events out. 'So you're saying that Mr Briggs is Charlie's father?'

Oleg laughed aloud. 'No, no, no,' he cried. 'Mr Briggs, as you call him, came later. Maureen didn't catch him until 2005.'

'You make her sound quite the femme fatale,' said Simon, who was really finding it hard to believe that Maureen Briggs was anything other than a suburban housewife. Were they really talking about the same person?

Tony wanted to know how Alina and Charlotte got on with each other. Oleg explained that after the separation, Maureen went to live with her mother, and it was there that she had the baby. Oleg saw nothing of Maureen and the child for several years, until about 2002. He told them how Maureen had called him and said she thought it only right that Alina should meet her sister.

'I was somewhat reluctant at first,' admitted Oleg, 'but eventually I agreed, and once a month Maureen took her daughters out for the day.'

'Where did they go?' asked Tony.

'Zoos, art galleries, museums, the usual places,' explained Oleg. 'You must understand that even from an early age the two girls were showing high levels of intelligence. After a year of these casual once-a-month meetings, Alina asked if Charlotte could come to the house and spend weekends with us. I was not happy, but thought, well they are siblings, I am now happily remarried, why not? My one condition was that Maureen brought Charlotte to the house, handed her over to my wife or to Olga, and then left. She was not to enter the house.'

'And how did the girls get on?' pushed on Tony.

'Fine, at first.' Oleg smiled. 'They had much in common. They loved me telling them Russian folk stories, which they were really much too old for.'

'You said at first?' added Tony.

'Indeed, at first everything was good. But then I began to notice jealousy emerging. Not from Alina, but from Charlie, a sort of spiteful resentment.'

'Can you give an example?'

'If I were telling a story and Alina put her arm around me, or tried to sit on my knee, Charlie would try to push her off. They were fine when I was not there, but as soon as I entered the room, things changed. It was as though they were both vying for my affection.'

'No doubt they were,' agreed Tony. 'So what happened?'

'In 2005 Maureen remarried and Charlotte's visits stopped.' Oleg sipped his tea. 'I can't say I was upset. It seemed that the family nurturing had come to a natural end.'

'You didn't see again her until when?' asked Tony.

'Not until 2017,' remembered Oleg. 'By this time, Alina was working as a junior lecturer in my department.'

'You're obviously proud of her,' put in Simon.

'Of course,' said Oleg. 'An aspiring academic. Anyway, one day in 2017, Alina entered my office with a striking young woman. "Look who I found in the student bar," she said. It was Charlotte, now a 20-year-old student in her last year at the Chelsea college. She informed me that she was changing direction and starting at Nottingham University, reading politics, in September. I congratulated her and made some useless quip, something like I hope they teach you about Russian politics.'

'How did she react?' asked Tony.

'Strangely. She smiled and said that if they didn't, she was sure that her mother would. I was taken aback by the remark. It was, I think, the first time I had ever heard her mention her mother. I told her that her mother was a fine academic.'

She said that she believed so, and that it was a pity the two of us couldn't have made a go of it.

'And your reply was?'

'Things are as they are. Alina sensed an atmosphere and announced that Charlotte was joining her for lunch with a friend at the newly opened brasserie in Russell Square. I said that I hoped they enjoyed it, and they left.

'In all the times that you met Charlotte, did she ever ask who her natural father was?'

'Never.'

'And do you know?'

'It was a long time ago. I have blocked it out of my memory.' At this point, Oleg stood up as a signal for them to depart. But he could not resist the last word.

'You ask many questions,' he said. 'Please allow me to ask one of you.'

'Certainly,' smiled Tony.

'Do you not remember me, young Ali Assad? Your father and I were great friends. We worked on many projects together. I have been to your house many times and met your gracious mother. You could only have been about five.' Tony was confused and puzzled. Why had Oleg suddenly brought this up?

'As you said,' smiled Tony. 'It is many years ago, and I do not remember.'

'Of course, why should you?' He shook hands and greeted him Salaam Alaikum. Tony responded, and was about to leave, when he turned into the room again, and looked at the picture.

'I was wrong,' he said. 'It's not monks coming out of cloisters, but spacemen. A sort of Brave New World.'

'If only it were,' smiled Oleg.

Chapter 13

After the interview, Simon dropped Tony at the office and made his way to suburbia to meet up, once more, with the contradiction that was Maureen Briggs. When he arrived at the house, the door was opened by Brian. 'I'm afraid Maureen's upstairs getting ready. Will it be a long visit?'

'No,' replied Simon, and was invited into the lounge. Brian said he would tell Maureen that Tony was there and went out. Left alone, Simon took the chance to look around the room. It was unremarkable, apart from there being no family photos. There was very little of a personal nature. Maureen entered. The change from the first time Simon had met her was remarkable. She was no longer a frumpy, prim woman. A striking and sophisticated lady met his eye.

'I'm sorry to disturb you,' started Simon.

'Not at all,' she replied. 'Brian's taking me out for a meal and to the theatre as a birthday treat.'

'Happy birthday,' responded Simon.

'It's next week, but the play won't be on then. Touring company, you know.'

'Mrs Briggs, when I last visited you, you failed to mention that you had another daughter,' began Simon.

She smiled and responded sharply. 'I don't remember your asking me.' Simon felt he had been quietly, but politely, put in his place. 'The fact is, if you must know,' she continued. 'I had three daughters. My eldest was born in 1988, and I called her Olga. I had the romantic idea that if I had children, I would name them after the three sisters in Chekov's play, Three Sisters, which is the play we are seeing tonight.'

'Three sisters?' asked Simon.

Maureen suddenly went still, and her cheerful mood vanished. 'Olga, my eldest daughter,' explained Maureen, 'died of meningitis before she reached her first birthday.' She stopped and took a deep breath. 'I decided then,' she went on, 'that the idea of using Chekhovian names was foolish. Olga, Maria, Irina, so Russian, don't you think?' She was reflecting on the past, what actually happened, and what could have happened.

Simon realised that he was addressing a deeply unhappy woman, but he had to persist with his questioning. 'Do you ever see your other daughter, Alina?'

'Of course I do,' replied, Maureen, pulling herself together. 'She stayed here for the last three nights.'

Simon's heart lifted. 'May I speak with her, please?'

'I'm afraid not. She left first thing this morning, and I doubt she'll be returning.' Simon looked at her. 'She took all her bags.'

'Have you any idea where she may have gone?' asked Simon.

'Sorry, no,' smiled Maureen. 'Alina is a very strong-minded girl. She will only tell you what she wants you to know.'

There was a voice from the hall, telling Maureen that she had to come, as the taxi was there, and the table was booked.

'I'm sorry,' apologised Maureen. 'I can't tell you anymore.'

Simon left, and decided to return to the office to report his findings to Tony.

***

When he got back, the office was a buzz of activity. Tony had been given the go-ahead. Laughing for the first time in a few days, he told Simon how Mark, Dame Edna, had given him the news. 'I've just spoken to the foreign secretary. What a panicker he is,' mimicked Tony, attempting an Australian accent. He continued in his own voice. 'But he's agreed to the decoy idea.' He gave Simon details of the plan. 'The real plane will arrive at Brize Norton sometime on Thursday evening. I wasn't given a time. But I was told that the envoy would be driven directly to Chequers to meet the Prime Minister and Mother Hubbard. It was suggested that the decoy plane should land at Stanstead at 1 am Friday morning, and that I tell my contacts I was unable to discover the location the envoy would be taken to.'

'That's bound to force a confrontation to take place at the airport itself,' responded Simon.

'Yes,' agreed Tony. 'Risky, I know, but workable, I believe. We've been given the task of liaising with the special forces unit.'

After he had spoken to Simon, Tony rang the imam he had spoken to the night before, and who had given him his contact number. The imam seemed pleased with the information and agreed to meet him at the Haroun Al Rashid at 7 pm the following evening.

For the rest of the day, Tony busied himself with organising the brief, and speaking to a somewhat off-hand officer from the special operations unit. The officer was not at all pleased with the strategy, or the tactics, but agreed to put the plan into action.

By 5 pm, Tony was beginning to feel the pressure of the day. Simon offered to take him to his house again, but Tony refused. 'No,' he said. 'I must overcome my concerns, and sleep in my own flat tonight.' Simon accepted this argument and left.

Tony realised that he was rather hungry, and decided that, rather than cook for himself, he would go to his local Indian restaurant. He ordered the special Madras with pilau rice, a couple of poppadoms with pickles, and a naan bread to soak up the sauce. He also ordered a pint of ice-cold lager.

After finishing the meal, he took a slow stroll home, and, though he dreaded entering the flat, he did so with a sense of confident determination. *This has to be done,* he thought, *so I'd better get on and do it.* Once inside, he poured himself a large whisky, sat on the sofa, watched a bit of television, had another glass and was soon asleep.

***

Robert was becoming less tense, less apprehensive. He was now in a state of mind where he could take in the room in which he was incarcerated. It appeared to be a warehouse of some sort. He had a basic bed. There was a small, makeshift kitchen where he could make coffee or tea whenever he wished. There were no ropes or chains restraining him. But he could not leave the room in which he was held. In front of him sat a young man of about twenty called Abdul, who prepared Robert's food on a basic electric cooker. The food was always North African, and always contained couscous. Lamb with couscous, chicken with couscous, but always couscous. Abdul was conscious of Robert's needs, and considerate regarding his situation. Yes, Abdul was a pleasant, cheerful boy, who was forever asking Robert questions. One such question took Robert completely by surprise.

'Are you a bitch boy?' he asked.

'A what?' replied the shocked Robert.

'A bitch boy.'

'I'm not sure what you mean,' responded Robert.

'A bitch boy. I am, at least I was.' He smiled. 'For my sister,' he added by way of explanation.

Robert looked mystified. 'You've lost me.'

'I was a bitch boy for my sister before she was married. Hakim, the man she was to marry, would come every night to see her. He would buy her presents, hold her hand, you know what I mean?' Robert nodded. 'Before he left, he would visit me in my bedroom and do to me what he was unable to do to my sister.'

Robert was taken aback. 'Oh, are you trying to tell me that you were gay?'

Abdul was most indignant. 'I am not, what you say, gay. I am not a queer. What I did was to preserve my sister's honour. It was my duty. Once they were married, he did not visit me again. When I marry, I will have a bitch boy to prepare me for my wedding night.'

'I thought that to lie with another man was against the Muslim belief,' said Robert.

'It is, if you mean it, if you enjoy it. But not if it's a duty.'

'A bit like the Ancient Greeks,' observed Robert.

It was now Abdul's turn to look confused.

Robert looked again at his gaoler. He was no longer scared of this little boy. He may have been twenty, but he was still a little boy, naive and immature, but kind and thoughtful. Could a boy like this really become a mercenary killer?

'Have you ever been to North Africa?' asked Abdul.

'No, I can't say that I have,' replied Robert.

'It is very different from here,' continued the boy. 'It is hot and dry, and the people are very...' He tried to think of the word.

'Passionate?' said Robert, trying to help him out.

'Passionate?' said Abdul, again confused.

'Quick-tempered, fiery.' Robert demonstrated with his hands a sudden explosive movement.

'That is right.' Abdul laughed. 'Fiery. One moment everything is calm, and then someone says something, and whoosh!' Abdul copied Robert's demonstration. 'Fiery, they are on fire.'

Suddenly the door opened and in walked Oleg Rebrov. He was in a smart suit and was very genial. 'Our friend here has been entertaining you?' he asked.

'He has been a good company,' replied Robert, looking at Oleg slightly apprehensively.

'Today is Tuesday,' started Oleg. 'It is hoped that the deal will be completed by Friday morning, and you will be free to go.'

'What deal?' asked Robert.

'An international deal,' smiled Oleg. 'Nothing for you to concern yourself with. Your friend Tony has been most helpful.' With that, he left the room, and the boy continued his friendly banter.

***

The following morning, Tony was in the department by 8.30 sorting out last-minute arrangements, when everything was turned on its head. The telephone rang and Felicity told Tony it was Chief Inspector Bullock. *What the hell could he want,* thought Tony, but went over to the phone and spoke politely.

'You'd better get your arse over here,' cried Bullock. 'One of your witnesses has been shot.'

'Who?' asked Tony.

'Charlie Briggs, the girl with the workshop. She's lying here dead in her Hounslow flat. Two bullets in her chest.'

Tony felt shock run through his body. 'Okay,' he said. 'I'll be there as soon as I can.' He put the receiver down, told Simon briefly what had happened, and asked him to join him on a visit to the crime scene.

***

The news of Charlotte's death was a shock to Oleg Rebrov. He was not upset, but confused and angry. 'Why? Who?' he cried. He had been told that she had been shot by a Russian Drotik pistol at close range. It had all the marks of a Russian assassination, but why? *What could she possibly have known that would warrant her death? Would Maureen know?*

No, he dismissed it from his mind. She couldn't possibly be involved in Charlotte's death. He wanted to call her and speak to her in Russian but knew that was not possible.

***

Simon was with the pathologist. 'A Drotik pistol, you say, one in popular use with the KGB?' The pathologist nodded in answer to Simon's question.

'How the hell?' asked Tony, as he knelt over the dead girl. Bullock handed him a photo. 'Know him?' he asked.

'Yes, I know him,' acknowledged Tony. 'But why would a photo of Kamel Ghaffar be in her possession?'

'There's a Russian connection,' stated Simon.

'Indeed, and there are two persons of interest who speak the language, and that is why I am joining you for the unpleasant job of informing Mrs Briggs that her daughter is dead.'

***

On hearing the news, Maureen Briggs remained still. No sign of distress, no sign of anger, no emotion. She was frozen, unable to take in the terrible news. Suddenly she changed, came out of her catatonic state, and spoke.

'I'm sorry. I didn't offer you a cup of tea.'

'That's okay,' replied Tony. 'Maybe your husband would like to make one for you.'

'Yes, of course,' said Brian, and headed for the kitchen. Mrs Briggs went into the lounge and sat down. She was again

Mrs Suburbia, all prim and correct. She obviously felt comfortable in that role.

It was difficult, but Tony had to speak to her. 'Mrs Briggs,' he began. 'Your daughter was shot by a Drotik pistol. Have you heard of such a pistol?'

'No,' she replied. 'Why should I have heard of it?'

'It is a Russian pistol,' replied Tony.

Maureen suddenly made the connection. 'I speak Russian,' she said assertively. 'I have studied the works of Russian writers: Chekhov, Tolstoy, Dostoyevsky and Pasternak. I have studied the Russian culture and way of life. I know nothing about guns, be they Russian, American, or British.'

Simon spoke. 'You know nothing of their politics?'

Only what I read. I have a monthly subscription to the Novaya Gazeta. I like to maintain my Russian reading and speaking abilities. It took me a lot of hard work to achieve them, and I don't wish to lose them.'

Tony showed her the photo of Kamel Ghaffar. 'Do you know this man?'

She looked at it, and for the first time there was visible shock in her eyes. She started to shake as Briggs entered with her tea. He saw her distressed state and sprang to her aid. 'What the hell?' he cried. 'I think you have asked enough questions. I must ask you to leave and allow my wife to grieve.'

Simon broke the silence as he sat in the car with Tony, both thinking of the short but strange interview.

'I have never experienced a mother, on being told of the death of her child, accepting it with such stoic resilience,' started Simon.

'They had been separated for a long time,' added Tony.

'Yes but…'

'What disturbs me was her reaction to the photo of Kamel,' murmured Tony. 'There's something wrong here, and we're not seeing it.'

Chapter 14

It was 4 pm. Tony was to meet the Imam at seven, so he decided to go and touch base with the only Russian he knew.

Oleg was his usual charming self. He showed Tony into the large drawing room where he was having a rather generous vodka and tonic. 'My bourgeois indulgence,' he said. 'In Russia it would be straight vodka, but since living in the UK I have picked up the British habit of adding tonic. Would you care for one? I can also offer you a gin and tonic?'

Tony declined the offer. Oleg stood for a while and then spoke. 'So I suppose you are here to ask me about the death of my daughter's sister, and how she got shot with a Russian Drotik pistol?'

Tony was completely taken aback. 'How did you know it was a Russian pistol?' enquired Tony.

Oleg looked at him for a moment, and then asked Tony to sit down. 'Are you sure you wouldn't care for a drink?' Tony felt he was in for a long explanation, but still declined the offer.

'You know that up to a few years ago, I was head of Russian literature at the London University?' Tony nodded. 'What you may not know was that teaching was not my only job; indeed it was not my main job. That, which provides me with this lovely house in Kensington, has nothing to do with the university. No, Mr Assad, my main post is with the British Foreign Office, where I am their main translator of, and informant about, anything Russian. The secretary is told of major Russian developments, but it is I who have to scrutinise any Russian documents that may come his way. I also have to read Russian journals and papers to find out how the Russian people feel and to analyse those feelings.'

'And what do the Russian people feel?' asked Tony, with a somewhat cynical tone in his voice.

'The main interest of the majority of Russians,' replied Oleg, 'is exactly the same as that of people in the UK. Money, crime, health and education. Despite what Pravda or Izvestia may wish you to think, the Russian people have very little interest in world politics. I say all this because when anything of a Russian nature hits the official desk, such as a murder using a sophisticated Russian pistol, then I am informed. That, Mr Assad, is how I know about the gun being a Drotik.'

Tony was irritated. Not with Oleg, but with Mark, who must have known about Oleg's official position but had not informed him.

'With your knowledge of Russia and the Russian psyche, why do you think that your daughter's half-sister was murdered?' enquired Tony.

Oleg shrugged. 'I honestly have no idea; it makes no sense to me.'

'Was Charlotte interested in or involved with Russian politics?' persisted Tony.

'Not that I know of. You'll have to ask her mother.'

'What about her mother? Is she a Russian sympathiser?'

'She is sympathetic to the plight of the ordinary Russian, I believe. You must understand that I have not spoken to her for several years,' explained Oleg.

'But she was a student of yours. That's where you both met?' Oleg nodded. 'Was she interested then?'

'I remember that she wrote a very good paper on Stalin's purge of the Tartar Muslims in the 1950s. Apart from that, I cannot remember her being interested in Russian politics.'

Tartar Muslims, Russia, Ukraine; all ticked boxes in Tony's head, but he let it rest for the moment. 'Tell me, Mr Rebrov,' asked Tony. 'As you are so well informed, through the Whitehall mafia, were you aware of my position in an operation which appears more of interest to MI6 than to MI5?'

Oleg answered, 'If you mean do I know you are the go-between regarding documents being flown in from the USA to the British government, yes I know that.'

'Why are these papers not being transmitted electronically?' asked Tony.

'Too sensitive. The Americans believe the British system to be compromised. Which incidentally it is, but then so is the American one.'

'And do you know what the documents contain?'

'If I knew what they contained, there would be little point in them being sent. I do, however, know what they are about.'

'Which is?' enquired Tony, who was becoming more interested in the second.

'Several North African countries are preparing for elections in the coming months. It is most important for the West to make sure the right candidates are empowered. Candidates who are, to some degree, sympathetic to the West's needs. We, that is the British, are of course aware of who these candidates are. The question is not who, but how. How does the American administration plan to install the right man into the right position of power?'

'You mean regime change?'

'For want of a better word, yes.'

'And what of Russia? Are they not interested?'

'Indeed yes,' smiled the Russian. 'Ever since perestroika and glasnost in 1986, the Russians have been losing world influence. Fear of not being a major world player encouraged Putin to make it his mission to develop a Russian place on the world stage. The area he is looking at, for such a development, is the Middle East, with its lucrative oil wells. Mr Putin, due to his own less than good position on human rights, finds that most of the countries in that area of the world, including Saudi Arabia, find it easier to discuss deals with him than with the West. They also appreciate his military support. This, of course, concerns the West, who rely on the area's oil resources.'

'What about the various Muslim countries?' asked Tony. 'Have they no say in the matter?'

'None. They are being squeezed, Mr Assad, squeezed by two world powers.'

'And what is your view?' asked Tony.

'I suspect it is the same as yours, Mr Assad,' replied Oleg. 'We may support British foreign policy on one level, but we feel it smacks of nineteenth-century colonialism. The British unfortunately have a very condescending attitude. They believe that what they do is for the good of a particular country, without fully understanding that country's needs. For the Russians, it is just a power base. If they secure the oilfields, they become world dictators. My sympathies are with the individual countries. Why cannot the East and the West leave them alone to make their own decisions?'

Tony agreed, and made a comment with which struck a chord with Oleg.

'Their trouble is their volatility.'

'Ah,' said Oleg. 'There's the rub.'

There was a silence while Oleg poured himself another drink. 'Mr Rebrov,' started Tony. 'May I come back to the real reason for my visit, which is the death of your daughter's half-sister?'

'Of course,' replied Oleg.

'You mentioned that the pistol was a Drotik. Have you any knowledge of this type of gun?'

'Indeed,' said Oleg. 'I own one.'

Tony was not surprised. He was past the point of being shocked. 'You know it is illegal to possess a gun in the UK?'

'I have a licence, issued through the Foreign Office,' smiled the Russian. 'In Russia, to own a gun is almost as common as it is in the United States of America. Only we don't have so many mass murders.'

'Could I see your gun, Mr Rebrov?' requested Tony.

'Of course,' replied Oleg. Using a key attached to his key ring, he unlocked a rather elegant Louis XVI cabinet. He pulled out an ordinary box and opened it casually. His face was, however, anything but ordinary when he discovered that the gun was gone.

'I do not understand!' he exclaimed. 'I just don't understand! I always keep the cabinet key on my keyring, and my keyring is always on my person'

'Do you have another key?' asked Tony.

'A spare key in a drawer in my dressing room.'

'May we take a look?' insisted Tony.

'Of course.' Oleg led Tony upstairs to the room which he called his dressing room. Compared to the rest of the house, it was very plain and basic. Rows of shirts, suits and jackets hung on rails, and there was a special rail for his many designer shoes. In the corner was a large 1920s chest of drawers. He pulled one drawer open and started rummaging. Letters, cards, old pen boxes, all the usual garbage one holds on to. He went through the drawers. In the bottom one were old electrical objects: an old torch, an electric razor that had seen better days and a lady's hair dryer. He exclaimed, 'Here it is! Here it is!' He held up a very old Babushka doll with chipped paint. He opened it and went through the various compartments. The fourth one unveiled what he sought: the key. 'Yes!' he exclaimed. 'Here it is.'

'And who knew of the key's existence in this room?' asked Tony.

'I'm not sure anyone did,' replied Oleg with a genuine look of puzzlement on his face.

***

Tony decided that before meeting the Imam, he would call at a local wine bar and have a large glass of Chardonnay and a chicken panini. He was not hungry; he simply wanted to calm himself down. He was angry. Angry with himself, and angry with the British government's complicity in what he considered colonial racism. He loved being English and was totally loyal to the crown, but he saw in the government's action a policy more in keeping with past years, when they used their power to subjugate other countries to their will. It was the world of the eighteenth and nineteenth century, with the armies of Catherine the Great of Russia claiming land which was not hers, and Lord Palmerston's gunboats trying to enforce our values and our laws on others. If it was not for Robert, he would have told Mark to hand the murder of Charlotte Briggs over completely to the Met, and the matter of the American documents to MI6, as they could be considered to be related to international terrorism. The terrorist in this case was, he considered, the American administration, supported by British foreign policy. That was what he wanted to say, but of course he could not while Robert was held captive. He had to play along, not because he agreed with what they were doing, but because of his love for Robert. Robert had to be the main focus of his attention, and he was becoming increasingly worried over Robert's possibly deteriorating mental state.

***

In fact, Tony had no need to worry. Robert not such a wilting violet as Tony thought. He was sitting with Abdul, eating yet another bowl of couscous, and talking about football, a subject about which he knew absolutely nothing.

Chapter 15

Tony entered the El Rashid at exactly 7 pm. It was empty apart from two men sitting at a corner table drinking coffee, and the imam sitting alone at the table usually occupied by him and his three brothers. Tony went over to him and sat down. After the usual salutations, the imam asked Tony what news he had. Tony told him that the plane from America was to land at Stanstead airport at 1 pm, but he could not find out the special envoy's destination.

'No matter,' said the Imam, looking into Tony's eyes. 'You're sure it's Stanstead?'

'Quite sure,' replied Tony.

'If the envoy were going to Chequers, which I am sure you would agree would be the most likely place for a meeting, then the plane would land at Brize Norton.'

Tony felt uncomfortable with this line of questioning but stuck to what he had said. 'Stanstead,' insisted Tony. 'Near London.'

'That is true,' replied the imam. 'And we have had confirmation from a different source that the landing is indeed Stanstead.'

Tony gave a sigh of relief.

'Nevertheless, Stanstead is an odd choice. Would you not agree?'

'I really haven't given it much thought.'

'But what if the authorities were tricking you?'

'In that case, they must be tricking your other source as well.'

'Very true, Mr Assad, very true,' smiled the Imam.

Tony was about to get up to go when the Imam indicated the two men sitting in the corner. 'You are now to stay with us until the operation is over.'

'That was not part of our deal!' exclaimed Tony.

'Things change,' explained the imam. 'Ali and Karim will take you upstairs where you will enjoy a good Lebanese meal with them and their brothers.'

Ali was young; he appeared to be about twenty. He smiled at Tony. 'Please come this way.' Tony followed. Karim said nothing.

The Imam spoke to the man behind the bar. 'You may open again for business, my friend.' He then left.

***

Earlier that day, Harry Morrell and Joe Langdon had been given the job of surveillance. It was no fun sitting in a car in a bleak and desolate car park, watching the door to a lock-up. The weather was wet, which was some compensation. Better than being on the beat, they thought, but would their shift ever end?

'Fancy popping down the street to the chippy and getting us a bag of chips?' asked Harry.

'Fuck off,' was the answer.

'I'll buy you some.'

'I could buy my own if I wanted some, which I don't. And I'm not leaving the warmth of the car on a wet day like today to get you some sodding chips. If you want some chips, go and get 'em yourself.'

Silence engulfed the car. The subject of chips was put on hold when they saw a man approaching the lock-up. They immediately sent a photo of him to MI5, and Harry asked if the office wanted them to intercept the man.

'No, stay as you are,' was Simon's order. 'We need them to believe that they are unobserved.'

The photograph was not very clear, but clear enough for Felicity to recognise the man as Kamel Ghaffar.

'Where is Tony?' demanded Mark, attempting authoritarianism.

'Went to see Oleg Rebrov, and then to the Haroun Al Rashid to keep his appointment with the Imam.'

'Why doesn't he answer his phone?' persisted Mark.

'He's more than likely switched his phone off, sir; these are delicate discussions,' replied Simon.

'I suppose you're right.' Mark returned glumly to his office.

***

It was past 8 pm when Ali and Karim brought in two large pizzas and a bowl of chips. 'I thought we were going to eat Lebanese food,' remarked Tony.

'You think in the Lebanon we don't have pizzas? Do you really think we are so backward?' remarked one of the men gruffly.

Ali, sitting opposite Tony, explained that it was pizza with a Lebanese topping

of goat's cheese, aubergine, onions, chicken, and herbs and spices.

'It tastes good,' commented Tony, not wanting another hostile remark from the gruff young man. The men ate hungrily, speaking in Arabic, unaware that Tony could understand every word. After they had finished eating, Karim said they were going for a smoke, and all left the room except Ali, who was left with Tony. Not wishing to let Ali know that he understood Arabic, Tony asked where the others had gone.

'They have gone for a cigarette,' replied Ali.

'You don't smoke?' Tony smiled.

'Yes, I do.' The answer was defensive, as though his manhood was in question.

'You come from North Africa?' the boy asked.

'Morocco,' Tony answered. 'At least my father came from Morocco.'

'What is your Moroccan name?' asked Ali.

Tony smiled. 'It is Ali, Ali Assad.' Tony had not used that name for many years.

The boy jumped up, overjoyed. 'You are called Ali. That is my name too, Ali Bettache'

'Not so remarkable,' commented Tony. 'Ali is a common enough name in Morocco.'

Then came the eternal questioning that North Africans love to do.

'Are you married?' asked the boy.

'No.'

'I am not married.' Then, as though to defend himself, 'I am a fighter.'

Tony smiled. 'That is good.'

Ali took a mobile out of his pocket and showed Tony photos of his family in Lebanon. 'That is my mother, my father, and this beautiful girl is my sister. She is called Yasmin.'

'A pretty name for a pretty girl,' agreed Tony.

'Yes. Yes, she is pretty.' He was pleased at Tony's response. 'She lives now in Lebanon, though we originally lived in Iraq.'

'Why did you leave Iraq?'

'The war,' replied Ali. Not wishing to pursue the subject, he went on to tell Tony that Yasmin was 13 years old. Next year she was to be married to Ali's uncle.

'How old is the uncle?' enquired Tony.

'Forty-five years of age. He is a good man, very rich. It's a good match,' answered Ali, with some pride.

'Lucky uncle,' commented Tony. 'Does your sister not mind that he is so much older than she is?'

'No, she is happy,' smiled Ali. It was at this point that the brothers' voices could be heard, shouting for Ali to join them. Ali got up. 'I must go,' he said. 'My brothers need me.'

Tony noticed that Ali had left his mobile in the room. He was about to shout and tell him that he had left it but decided against it. When the boy had gone, he picked up the phone and looked at the contacts. He found the name Yasmin and sent her a message in Arabic.

Not long after Ali had left, the door opened. To Tony's surprise, it was Oleg Rebrov.

'I dare say you are surprised to see me,' he said.

'Should I be?' asked Tony.

'I am here,' continued Oleg, 'for your protection. The brothers can become rather zealous in their actions. They are unaware of what a special person you are, Mr Assad.'

'So you're the different source the imam mentioned?' asked Tony. Oleg nodded.

'I don't understand you, Mr Rebrov. Whose side are you on?' asked Tony.

'The same as you, Mr Assad, the side of common sense.'

'You are Russian. Do I assume therefore that you are on the side of Russia?'

'Mr Assad, I am from Ukraine. I am a Tartar Muslim. Yes, officially I am a Russian citizen. But that does not mean that I like Russians.'

'I am confused,' admitted Tony.

'My father was born in 1910 in Sevastopol, Ukraine, part of the Crimean Peninsula.

My grandfather was a machine operator. I understand he was a very clever man. The family lived well in Sevastopol. Their situation would be what today would be called the middle class. In 1928 my father started training to be a teacher of English and qualified in 1931. Soon after that he met my mother and they married. Two years later my mother gave birth to a little girl. In 1939 my father enlisted in the Russian army and my grandfather, because of his electrical skills, was moved to a factory in Stalingrad. My grandmother was ordered to work in a munitions factory in Sevastopol. My mother, because she had a young child, was excused military service and did not have to work. My grandparents on my mother's side were sent to a work camp in Siberia. They died there. Their age made them susceptible to the effects of the cold and to disease. My mother never got over the loss, and bitterly hated and despised the people who had sent them there.

'After the war, my father and grandfather returned. Unfortunately, my grandmother on my father's side had not survived the hard labour. My mother was drained and exhausted, but she was still a young woman, and was strong and resilient. As a family, we had got through the war and we were all in one piece. It was shortly after my father's return from the war that Stalin began his purge on the Tartar Muslims, accusing them of being collaborators in the war. He ordered all Tartar Muslims to give up their rights of citizenship and leave what was then the USSR. My father, of course, protested. He had been a soldier fighting for Russia, and my grandfather had done more than most in the development of armaments. But the authorities would have nothing of it. They were told to move to Vladivostok. My father refused. He called Vladivostok the arse of the world. He purchased a van, and, with my mother, my grandfather, and my little sister, drove through the Dardanelles to Turkey. We ended up in Istanbul, where my father was able to get a job teaching English. It was, I understand, a hard time. The Turks were not exactly welcoming. My father swore he would not return to the Ukraine or Russia until Stalin was dead. And that's what happened. In the summer of 1952 Stalin was ill, and by 1953 he was dead. The laws relating to Tartar Muslims were relaxed, and my family returned to their home city of Sevastopol.

'My father soon obtained a job teaching English. The Russians hated the Americans, but they realised the importance of English as a subject in schools. English teachers were prised commodities in the Soviet education system.

'My parents resisted the notion of having children while in exile, but once they were back in Ukraine, I was born. I must have been a bright boy, for in 1972 I enrolled on a joint English and Russian literature course at the University of Kiev. Kiev was the capital of Ukraine.'

'English and Russian literature. That must have been hard work,' observed Tony.

Oleg smiled. 'Russian can be very heavy and turgid. Indeed the style of Russian literature has changed very little over the last thousand years, whereas English literature is vibrant and uplifting. English literature of the sixteenth century is different from that of the seventeenth, and that of the seventeenth different from that of the eighteenth. And as for the nineteenth century, the works of Hardy, Dickens, Austen and the Brontës made that a marvellous period.'

Tony wondered if he would ever stop waxing lyrical on the wonders of the English language, but he did.

'After I obtained my degree I returned to Sevastopol. My father was not in good health, and my mother had died two years earlier from cancer. 'Leave Russia,' my father said. 'It is a hateful place. We Muslims are not wanted. Go west,' he said, 'anywhere west.' So I started looking for international positions. Eventually one came up, a junior lecturer in Russian at the University of London. I applied and was called for an interview. I loved London from the moment I arrived and decided whether or not I got the job, I would stay. Well, as you must realise, I got the job and started working at the university. I must have done well because I was quickly promoted. Then one day I was called into the Dean's office.

He told me that the Foreign Office wanted someone to translate a number of Russian documents at speed, and the Dean asked me if I would be willing to take on the task. They were not difficult translations, but long and laborious. It took me two weeks to complete the full assignment. At the end of it the foreign secretary expressed his thanks, and said he was very impressed with the speed and accuracy of my translations. It was then that he came up with the suggestion that I be co-opted to the Foreign Office staff as an official translator to deal with anything Russian. So that's how I came to have two jobs.'

'You mentioned you had a sister,' said Tony.

'Yes, Sonia. She remained in Ukraine, moved to Kiev, and continued to hate the Russians. She died four years ago from a stroke. It was very sad.'

'Did you attend her funeral?' asked Tony.

'No, I swore when I left Russia that I would never return, and I never have.'

'That's some story,' commented Tony.

'You must wonder why I am here tonight, and why I tell you the story of my life.'

'I think I know,' replied Tony.

'The Imam does a wonderful job on the streets of London, helping the Islamic community in many ways. But the organisation that I and your father represent takes a far wider look at the evolving nature of world politics. We feel it incumbent on us to influence governments and political thinking on the Muslim world. It is, as has been said many times before, only a small planet where conflict and confrontation should have no place.'

'You speak very eloquently, Mr Rebrov,' said Tony. 'I suspect you are here on a mission to ask me to join your Muslim organisation, and though I agree wholeheartedly with what you say, I am not sure that I am your man.'

'It would make your father very proud of you.'

'I am not like my father,' replied a defiant Tony.

'I think you are very much alike.' There was a pause, and Oleg stood up to leave the room. 'Will you at least think about what I have asked?'

'Yes,' replied Tony. 'That's if we get out of this situation alive.'

'Oh, you'll get out alive, that I promise you, Mr Assad.' And with that, Oleg left the room.

Chapter 16

It was decided that, though he was no actor, Mike Bailey should take on the role of the American diplomat.

'You don't have to act; just get off the plane in a smart suit. You do have a smart suit, don't you?' asked Simon, to the amusement of those gathered. 'Get off the plane with a briefcase and get into a waiting limo.'

'What if they try to stop me?' complained Mike.

'Well, let's hope they do, otherwise this heist will have been a waste of time.'

Simon then became serious and addressed the whole room. This included, apart from MI5 staff, those recruited from special ops.

'The plane carrying Mike will fly from Robin Hood airport in Nottinghamshire to Stanstead, landing at 1 am. When Mike leaves the plane, two of you will be in front of him and two behind. You will be armed. You, Mike, as special envoy, will have a briefcase handcuffed to your wrist at all times. The limo has bulletproof glass, so once you're in there you're safe. The rest of you will be on the perimeter of the airfield, waiting for the plane to land.'

'How are the terrorists going to get into the airport?' asked Johnson.

'That's their problem,' replied Simon.

One of the special ops men asked how likely it was that they would see any action.

'Very likely,' was the answer. 'But keep the shooting to a minimum. We want these men in court, not dead. Well, good luck, gentlemen. We leave at precisely 11 pm.'

After dismissing the men, Simon went up to Felicity and asked if she had had any news from Tony. 'None,' she replied. 'And it's now 24 hours since he went to the Al Rashid.'

'Yes,' agreed Simon. 'My concern is that he's being held hostage.'

'He'll be okay, sir,' Felicity said, in what she hoped was a reassuring voice.

'Yes, I'm sure he will be.' He did not sound convinced. 'Now go and get yourself a coffee and some food. Then rest. The next few hours could be rather stressful.'

'Yes, sir.' And with that, Felicity left. Simon was about to take the advice he had given Felicity and have a coffee and a rest, when he was stopped by Mark.

'Heard from Tony?' asked Mark.

'No, sir. We suspect he's being held until the assignment is over.'

Mark shook his head. 'That may not work out well for Tony.'

'No, sir,' Simon agreed, and left the room.

***

Ignorant of their concerns, Tony was feeling pretty relaxed. He had been left alone all day, apart from Ali coming in and bemoaning the fact that he had lost his phone.

'Where do you think you may have lost it?'

'I do not know. Can you remember whether I had it when I left this room last night?' Ali asked.

'I'm sure you did,' lied Tony.

'I must have lost it when I went out to see my brothers. My brothers will secure me another one.'

Secure one, thought Tony. *I wonder what he means by that.* He decided it was wise not to ask.

At about three in the afternoon, the door opened and to Tony's surprise, it was Kamel.

'And how are you, my friend? Is Ali looking after you?'

'Everything is fine,' replied Tony. 'Though I can't quite get my head around the fact that everyone is being so nice, and yet I am being held hostage.'

'Just because you are being held, my friend, does not mean we cannot show you good hospitality. The brothers like you,' added Kamel.

'Oh, well, that is reassuring,' replied Tony.

'Tell me,' said Kamel. 'How did you find out that my name was Kamel?'

'Kamel,' answered Tony. 'And before that, David Green. Why the change?'

'I think you know why,' said Kamel, with a knowing smile. 'But my interest is how you fell upon my name in the first place?'

'Your name was linked to a case I was investigating eighteen months ago, where a priest was burnt alive in North Yorkshire.'

'Ah, yes, very unfortunate.'

'Is that all you can say, unfortunate?' responded Tony sharply.

'I had heard discussions about a plot against some foolish priest. I told them not to go ahead with it. They disregarded my advice, and in so doing, put me in the frame. It was unfortunate, but such things happen.'

'You make it sound like a game,' responded Tony.

'It is a game, and at the moment the West is winning. This year in the UK there have been fewer than 50 attacks, many of them far-right provoked. In Iraq or Lebanon, we are talking thousands.'

'I understand what you are saying.'

'Do you Tony, do you really? Your MI5 are doing a good job protecting the UK, but what of the people in the Middle East? Who's protecting them?'

'And what is your answer?' asked Tony.

'The West must step away and stop interfering with sovereign countries and their systems of law.'

'And the Russians?'

'Yes, them too. Iraq, Libya, Syria and Lebanon should all be ruled by their own governments.'

'Even if those have not been democratically elected?'

'Yes, even then. They know their country; they know their people. Give them the freedom to run it their way. No, the West may not like the things they do, but their interference makes matters far, far worse.'

Tony sighed. How many times had he heard such arguments from radical young Muslims? For Tony, it was a simplistic argument, full of flaws. Could we stand by during the 2nd World War while Hitler massacred the Jewish population? Could we stand aside in Uganda or Yugoslavia? These were moral questions with unpalatable answers.

After Kamel had finished his rant, he smiled. 'My apologies for getting overheated,' he said.

'No problem,' answered Tony.

'I get very worked up.'

'Yes,' agreed Tony. Kamel took a cigarette out and offered one to Tony.

'No thanks,' Tony replied. 'I don't smoke.'

'Arrangements for tonight,' started Kamel. 'You will come with me to Stanstead. We shall leave here at approximately 10:30 pm. That should give us plenty of time to get to the airport.'

'I am coming with you?' asked Tony, somewhat surprised.

'Certainly, you are. Why would you think you were not?'

Tony smiled. 'Of course,' he replied.

When Kamel had gone, Tony puzzled out the reason for them taking him with them. Surely it would make more sense for them to hold him here as hostage? They were Muslims, but very different from any jihadists he had had the misfortune to deal with in the past. What were they up to?

Chapter 17

At 1 pm the full team was assembled, apart from Mike Bailey. He had been driven by the police, with instructions to use the blue light if necessary, to Robin Hood airport, where he was to prepare himself for take-off at 12:30 pm. It would not be a long flight, and the pilot was instructed to circle Stanstead and land at exactly 1 am.

'Good to see you all,' started Simon. 'I hope you all feel rested and ready for what could be a night of surprises.'

Simon went over the plan, and then handed over to the sergeant in charge of special ops. The sergeant went over the rules of engagement in great detail. Firearms were to be used only as a last resort. For example, if their life or a colleague's life were in danger.

'Remember,' he said. 'No heroics. This isn't fucking Gunfight at the O.K. Corral.'

After the instructions were given, they were dismissed to find their transport, and the convoy set off. Simon and Roger Johnson were to set off later in a specially leased limo with darkened windows.

'We might as well go in style,' smiled Simon, and Roger agreed.

***

It might have been all excitement at MI5, but at the lock-up at Ruislip, it was deadly silent. The men doing surveillance had seen only the one appearance of Kamel Ghaffar, who stayed for a very short time. There was also the occasional appearance of a young Middle Eastern man, who kept coming out for a cigarette.

'Are they sure anything's going to happen?' moaned Joe Langdon.

'Ours not to reason why,' replied Harry.

'I hate jobs like this,' continued Joe, in his usual negative and somewhat irritating voice. 'I could be at home tonight watching tele; there's the Chelsea-Liverpool match on tonight.'

'Liverpool will win,' responded Harry.

'I'm not so sure,' replied Joe. 'Chelsea has got that new centre-forward from the Czech Republic.'

'Maybe,' said Harry. The banter went on until about midnight when a Fiat Mira arrived.

'Who the hell is this?' said Harry, sitting up, alert.

The car stopped and the lights went out. They sensed that the door was being opened. Someone got out and walked slowly to their car. Eventually, a woman arrived at the driver's side.

'You gave us a bloody shock,' they cried.

'Good to be kept alert,' responded Felicity. 'I've got the spare set of keys for the lock-up from Peacock's. Thought they might be useful.'

It was at this moment that Joe noticed Felicity's eccentricity: her dyed red hair, large glasses, and bright red and orange clothes. In the office she was known as Miss OCD, because of her careful and methodical attention to detail. She chirped like a bird.

'Mind if I sit in the back and join you boys?'

'Not if the boss doesn't mind,' said Joe. The distraction was most welcome.

'By the boss, if you mean Tony, he is, we believe, being held hostage.'

'Bloody hell,' cried Joe. 'Who's holding him? The terrorists?'

'No, bloody Mickey Mouse, you dickhead,' carped Harry at Joe's moronic response.

This light-hearted banter, though funny, took their attention away from their main focus. They did not notice a young girl cycle up to the unit. She had no lights on and was wearing dark clothes. They did not see her dismount, leave the cycle, and enter the unit. Their lack of attention was to have consequences.

*****

It was 8 pm when Tony was ordered to get ready. He was told that the car was there, and he was to prepare himself for a long journey.

'What,' cried Tony. 'It's only 8 pm.'

There was no reaction to this statement. He was pushed out of the room by one of the brothers. When he got outside, he saw a large maroon BMW with its rear windows blacked out. He did notice that the driver of this luxury car was Kamel Ghaffar. He was pushed into the back and the other men got into a van to follow them. Tony was not alone in the back of the car. There was a tall, good-looking man, whom Tony estimated to be in his thirties and from Sudan.

'Good evening, Mr Assad,' the man said. 'I have heard so much about you that I almost feel I know you.' He smiled. 'The name is Osman Brown.'

'And why are you here?'

'Let's say I have an interest in what you are doing tonight.'

'Well, if you have an interest,' rebuked Tony, 'why are you here at 8 pm, five hours before the expected landing at Stanstead?'

'That, Mr Assad, is because we are not going to Stanstead.'

'We're not?' Suspicion rising in Tony's voice.

'No, Mr Assad, we thought it better for us to take a trip out to Brize Norton. Kamel estimates it to be a two-hour journey if he drives at a good speed.'

'But even so,' interjected Tony.

'Even so,' said a confident Osman smiling, 'you think I will be too early. Certainly early for an 1 am arrival, but not one at 10:30 pm, which is the official time that the special envoy will be arriving at Brize Norton.'

Tony was shocked and felt a raging despair hit the pit of his stomach. He sat back and was thinking what he should do when Osman suddenly produced a gun.

'You like the gun?' asked Osman. 'It's a Beretta 9000 pistol. I take it that as a special agent you know how to use such weapons?'

Tony said nothing.

'I take it from your silence,' Osman continued, 'that you do, which is just as well. For tonight, Mr Assad, I want you to greet the American diplomat, shake hands with him, and then shoot him in the head. Bang!'

Osman made the sound of a gun being fired.

'But why? Why use me as your assassin?' Tony replied, with real panic in his voice.

'For the simple reason that you're not an assassin, and therefore won't arouse any suspicion. I might add, Mr Assad, that if you do not do it, your friend will be shot. But don't worry, you won't have to mourn him, as you will also be dead.'

Tony was stunned. He did not know what to say or do. How the hell was he going to get out of this situation?

It was early evening and the roads were quiet, so it did not take long to drive down the Edgeware Road and on to the M1. It was not until they hit the motorway that Tony spoke again. He had felt from the moment he had got into the car that there was something wrong about this man. With Kamel, and Ali and his brothers, there was a passion. They were on a mission, a crusade. But not this man; he was too much in control.

'All this for political ideals,' Tony said. 'All about who will rule in Damascus, Tripoli and Baghdad.'

'It means a lot to them,' replied Osman, with contempt in his voice.

'But not to you?' asked Tony.

'No, not to me,' agreed Osman, in a matter-of-fact way.

'Then why?' asked Tony. 'Why are you involved in a project that you have so little interest in?'

'Ah, that is where you are wrong,' replied Osman. 'I have an interest, a very keen interest, but not in elections. You see, Mr Assad, as well as the documents relating to the election, there is also another plan which I am most interested in.'

'And what is that?' asked Tony.

'It is an agricultural dossier relating to the restructuring of land in Afghanistan, and that,' he said forcefully, 'cannot be put into effect.'

'No?' asked Tony.

'No, absolutely not. You must understand, Mr Assad, that I have a major distribution network based on the annual agricultural turnover in Afghanistan. It is worth millions.'

'You mean drugs.' Tony was now beginning to understand.

'I mean heroin, Mr Assad, a product that keeps me rich and the British economy vibrant.'

By now they were travelling through the Oxfordshire countryside, and Tony was still no nearer to a solution.

They arrived at Brize Norton at roughly 10 pm, and using forged documentation were able to get onto the airfield where the car took up a position as the official limo for the diplomat. The van parked a little way behind them, and the men took their places. At 10:30 pm there was the sound of an aeroplane coming in to land, and then the flashing lights on its wings could be seen. It taxied along the runway and slowly came to a halt. The engine was cut. The door to the passenger cabin remained closed. Steps were brought to the crew door, and the plane's crew came out, but no diplomat. The door remained closed. The crew began to walk to the main building, leaving just a service engineer to secure the plane. One of Osman's men went up to him.

'Was this a private flight from the US?' he asked.

'What?' said the engineer, looking both surprised and shocked. 'This plane is a return flight from Belfast.'

'No passengers?'

'No, why should there be. It was simply a return of a plane.'

'Are there any other landings tonight?' continued the man.

'Not that I'm aware of, why? Say, you're asking a lot of questions, who the hell are you?'

With that, the engineer was shot in the head with a silenced gun.

Osman was not happy and instructed the gang to make for Stanstead.

'It's not eleven yet, and if we drive at a good speed, we should make Stanstead before 1 am.'

The tone of the words demonstrated Osman's great irritation.

Chapter 18

George Mathers and John Stanley were security guards at Stanstead airport. They manned Gate Two at the airport. This gate allowed fuel tankers to access the airport. Both men took their jobs very seriously. They were surprised when, that evening, they were asked to present themselves at one of the many private offices in the main airport block. On arrival at the office, they were greeted by the head of airport security and senior officers from MI5. They were told that there was an operation going ahead that night in which they, indirectly, were going to be involved. The MI5 officer explained that at 11:10 pm a unit of special ops men and MI5 officers would arrive. They would show the guards documentation, examples of which were produced, and they were told to open the gates for these men.

'The tricky bit,' explained the officer, 'is that somewhere between 12 pm and 1 am, another group of vehicles will arrive. We don't know exactly when. They will also ask for permission to enter. They may have forged documentation. We do not know. What you must do is question them and challenge their authority. It is important that you do this, otherwise you'll arouse their suspicions. Once you have done this convincingly, you must let them in. Needless to say, you must not tell anyone what has been discussed here tonight. Do you understand?'

The two men understood and felt full of heroic bravado as they returned to the guardhouse to take on their night shift.

Osman's car arrived at one of the side gates to Stanstead Airport at 12:40 am. One of Osman's men got out of the car, went to the guard on duty, and showed him the documentation he had used at Brize Norton.

'Sorry, mate,' George replied. 'No can do. For me to let you in it must be an official Stanstead document. I mean, be fair, anyone could have written this.'

'No,' said the man. 'Look again. It's an official government document.'

George looked at it again. 'It's more than my life's worth to let you in.'

'Really,' smiled the man. 'Your life's not worth a great deal anyway.'

With that he shot the guard between the eyes, a good clean shot. John, who had been sorting paperwork at the back of the office turned and was quickly despatched with one direct shot. The shooter, showing a complete lack of feeling, calmly walked inside the guardhouse and lifted the gates, allowing Osman's convoy to enter. Special ops and the men from MI5 had been there a good hour and a half. They were getting bored but were very tense. Fred Willis and Jack Brownly, both from special ops, were dressed as maintenance engineers appearing to work on a plane near to where the target plane would land. Both men were fully prepared to take action once the landing had been completed. Other special ops were dotted around the airport, but an open field made for difficult surveillance. Everyone braced themselves as Osman's car entered the area. It entered just as the plane was coming in to land. It was driven to the same position as at Brize Norton. The plane taxied to a halt, and steps were pushed up to the fuselage to allow passengers to disembark. The Beretta was put into Tony's hand, and a gun placed against his head.

'Now it is your turn, Mr Assad,' said Osman threateningly.

The car door was opened, and Tony climbed out. He walked to the plane in a mindless daze, followed by one of Osman's men holding cutters to cut the steel handcuffs which held the briefcase to the diplomat's wrist. It was not a long walk, but it felt like an eternity. Through the corner of his eye, he saw Ali, wild with excitement. Ali, on his lonely walk, took in the whole airport: the planes and the control tower. He was young and this was a real adventure. When Tony got to the steps that led to the plane's interior, he saw the American envoy coming down. It was Mike Bailey wearing a smart suit, and with a big surprised smile on his face. Tony could feel the cold steel of the weapon inside his pocket. There was no way he was going to use it. Could he call to Mike to hold up his document case so he could shoot into it? No, that might work in the movies, but not in real life. If he turned around and shot at the gangster holding the cutters, he would immediately be mowed down by the other members of the gang. Then the tragedy happened. The tragedy that no one could have foreseen. Ali, the young man, who had sat for two days with Tony in his prison cell, suddenly saw one of the special ops men. He realised it was a set-up, jumped up, and ran forward, shouting that it was a trap. That was it. There was an explosion, smoke came from the special ops officer, and Ali lay on the floor.

'No!' cried Tony, turning and running to the boy. By this time, the Muslim brothers, supported by the mob, had opened fire on the special forces. Tony ran to Ali, who was lying on the floor with blood coming from his lifeless body. Suddenly Tony felt an arm on his shoulder.

'There's nothing you can do,' said Roger Johnson, and forced him into the official limo where Simon was sitting with a can of lager.

'Sorry it's not champagne,' he said. Tony was in no mood for jokes.

'We've just killed an innocent lad. He was a good person, a nice boy.'

'There's nothing you can do, Tony,' said Simon. Tony knew it was the truth. The car sped out of the airport and hit the M1 on its way to London.

It must have looked almost comical: two limos racing down the motorway. It could have come out of a Carry-On film, but the driver of the limo was not Charles Hawtry, and there was nothing funny about the situation.

In the BMW, Osman had been on the phone since leaving the airport. Suddenly he spoke.

'At the next service station, I want you to pull in,' he ordered.

'I can't do that,' argued Kamel.

'I'm afraid you will, Mr Ghaffar,' and a Beretta was aimed at the Muslim's head.

'But they'll catch up with us.'

'No, we had a good start on them. I will get out, you will drive on, and they will follow you.'

Kamel could see Osman's selfish logic. He was going to save his own skin at all costs. Kamel had no alternative but to comply with the demand. He pulled into the service station and Osman got out. He had obviously arranged for a car to collect him. He got out and disappeared like a thief in the night. Kamel immediately raced out of the service station, his one thought being to get to the lock-up and use Robert as a bargaining chip. Risky, he knew, but he had few other choices.

It was nearly 2 am when the BMW raced into the yard which housed the lock-up. The surveillance team had been thinking he would never come when he arrived and screeched to a stop. *Ah*, thought the men, *was this going to be their moment?* Kamel jumped out of the car and raced to the lock-up. Joe and Harry got out slowly, preparing to follow him, when the big limo containing Tony came in. Tony was out and running to the lock-up. He entered and suddenly stopped. There was silence. Kamel was standing there, no movement, hardly breathing. In front of him stood a girl holding a Drotik pistol. The girl started to speak quietly, defiantly.

'She was always jealous. I remember as a little girl she resented our house and the way we lived, but most of all she resented me having a father. If she could have taken him away from me, I am sure she would. Then our mother remarried. She had a father and with that, she disappeared. I didn't meet her again, not properly, until I was in my early thirties. She was in her twenties, and foolishly I introduced her to you. To my boyfriend, and the same green flame burned in her heart. She wanted you for herself.'

'Alina, it was not like that,' cried Kamel.

'Then how was it, you tell me?'

There was silence, and then suddenly another voice, Maureen's voice.

'I was in my mid-thirties, married to a highly successful lecturer,' she explained. 'We had everything: money, a nice house, and good clothes. It may have been material goods, shunned by Oleg's contemporaries in Russia, but we loved it. We were happy. We had a lovely child. Nothing seemed able to touch us until one day in came a young, good-looking student. He was energised, with views and attitudes which excited me. We talked. I engaged with his ideas. Foolishly, I allowed myself to fall in love. Sadly, that partnership had consequences.'

Alina fell on her knees, stunned to hear this.

Kamel spoke quietly. 'Charlie wasn't my lover,' he explained. 'She was my daughter.'

'You mean I killed my own sister for no reason? No! No! I won't hear it.' She put her hands over her ears. She was led out of the lock-up by Felicity, who took her to a waiting patrol car.

'Kamel Ghaffar,' started Tony, 'you will need to come with us.'

'Why?' he asked.

'You know why,' replied Tony. 'If for no other reason than that there is a young boy lying dead on the runway at Stanstead airport.'

'I did not kill him,' protested Kamel.

'I know that, but you bear some responsibility.'

'The English forces shot that boy and he lies dead on the floor, the same as many such boys do where I come from. Shot by the West but engineered in such a way that Islam takes the blame. What you saw tonight was nothing more than a microcosm of what happens every day, every night, in the countries of the East.'

Kamel was led away. Tony felt sad and deflated. Guilty at the part he had played in this awful charade. However, his spirits were suddenly lifted when an arm was put around his shoulders, and Robert spoke in a pleading voice.

'Please, whatever is cooked in future, no more bloody couscous.'

Tony smiled weakly, and they left the lock-up to the forensic team.

Chapter 19

When Tony entered MI5 the following morning, everyone was in high spirits, congratulating each other and slapping each other on the back. Tony, however, was far from happy. He was upset and angry and knew that he would have to have it out with Mark.

'So what's bitten your arse?' asked Mark, as Tony entered his office.

'I am upset and fucking angry,' complained Tony.

Mark realised there was going to be a confrontation and told Tony to shut the door and take a seat.

'So,' began Mark. 'Care to tell me why you are so upset?'

'Sure,' began Tony. 'I'm upset because I was driven through the Oxfordshire countryside at gunpoint to Brize Norton. You remember, Mark, that is the airport where the American diplomat was supposed to land. The only problem was timing. I understood the landing to be at 1 am, and my abductors thought it was 10:30 pm. It turns out the 10:30 pm plane was an internal flight from Belfast, and no other plane was scheduled for landing that night. So we were all wrong. My question is, how did the men who were holding me know about Brize Norton, and where the hell was the American diplomat?'

'I don't know,' answered Mark casually. 'I know that the American arrived by scheduled flight from Washington on Wednesday morning, had dinner with the PM that evening, and returned to America the following day. I have no idea why this Osman character decided to take an excursion to Brize Norton. It doesn't make sense. Unless someone was trying to divert him from Stanstead. If that is so, then why? And to be honest, Tony, I have no answer.'

'Why was I not informed that the American diplomat had already arrived?' insisted Tony.

'We thought it may compromise the operation. Remember, what we wanted was to catch the men who were holding your friend, and, most importantly, to rescue him from whoever held him prisoner.'

Tony couldn't argue with this, but still felt disgruntled that he had not been informed.

When eventually he returned to his desk, he was still confused and bewildered. Who would want to sabotage the operation? Who would gain from the wild goose chase to Oxfordshire, unless they believed that the information they held on the landing time was correct? And then it struck him. What if someone knew that the real documents were coming into Brize Norton, and wanted the West's ground plans for the Middle East to be seen by the Muslim brotherhood? Who would gain from such a strategy? Oleg. Of course, it had to be Oleg who had tipped off Osman. But did he get the timing wrong? No. It was the British who got it wrong. They assumed that because the flight to Stanstead was landing at 1 am, the one to Brize Norton would be landing at the same time. Oleg had been fed the wrong information. He had been told that the plane with the documents would land at 10:30

155

pm. He assumed that was a trick, and the documents were indeed coming to Stanstead, not knowing that the plans were already with the prime minister. If that was the case, Oleg's information had been compromised. In Tony's confused mind, things started to clear. Oleg was a Russian, whether he liked it or not. He would have been brought up in a culture where revenge was taken for hurt pride. Charlotte was the result of his hurt pride. Kamel was the one who had seduced his wife, which made Kamel the object of his revenge. Oleg knew about the relationship between Kamel and Charlie, yet refused to say anything. Instead, he allowed Alina to build up a passionate Russian hatred towards someone she felt had betrayed her. And then at the right moment, he placed a Drotik in her hand. It was clear now, and Tony felt sick.

***

After a much-needed coffee and a debriefing with his team, Tony set off for the Haroun Al Rashid. It was not a journey he wanted to make, but he knew he had to.

By the time he got to the bar, it was afternoon, and Friday prayers were over. The café was full, but it went quiet when he entered. It was an eerie, threatening silence. At the bar, he ordered mineral water, and then walked over to the table where the Imam sat.

'I am surprised to see you here today, my friend,' said the imam.

'I had to come. I had to express my sorrow for the way yesterday evening turned out, and to pass on my condolences concerning young Ali.'

'We are used to such deaths,' remarked the imam. 'But we are not used to betrayal.'

'I did not betray you.' Tony passed Ali's phone to the Imam. 'You will note that he texted his sister, saying how proud he was, and giving her times and details of the plan.'

The Imam read the text.

Dear Sis, I am going to be a hero. At 1 am British time we are going to attack an American envoy at Stanstead airport which is some way from London. If I die in this expedition, be proud of me, for I will have died a martyr to the cause of Islam. Your loving brother Ali.

The Imam put the phone down and looked at Tony.

'I understand Ali lost his phone.'

'He found it in the room where I was held. Just before he left, he handed it to me and told me he was not allowed to take it with him in case the authorities tracked him.'

'So,' continued the Imam. 'He understood the concept of tracking, and so would know that a text to his sister would be intercepted.

'Would know,' explained Tony, 'must be replaced with should know. He was excited; it was his first mission. He wanted to tell someone; is that so hard to believe?'

'Maybe.' The Imam was unconvinced.

'Here's my card,' said Tony. 'It may be of some use in times to come.'

He stood up. 'If, in future, you run any fundraising events for the Muslim community, let me know, my friend and I will willingly come along and donate.'

He turned and left the bar, hoping Ali would forgive him for making him out to be culpable for the aborted mission.

Tony had to believe that what he had done was for the greater good.